A Book of
Bargains

Vincent O'Sullivan

With a frontispiece by Aubrey Beardsley

Solis Press

Also by Vincent O'Sullivan and available
from Solis Press: *The Good Girl*

Originally published in 1896 by Leonard Smithers in London.
This edition completely reset with minor spelling changes and
published in 2014 by Solis Press

Typographical arrangement copyright © 2014 Solis Press
Photographs © 2014 Robert Gray

ISBN: 978-1-910146-02-6

Published by Solis Press, PO Box 482,
Tunbridge Wells TN2 9QT, Kent, England

Web: www.solispress.com | *Twitter*: @SolisPress

Contents

Aubrey Beardsley's frontispiece drawing from the original edition.
"The Business of Madame Jahn" [page 37]

THE FIRST BARGAIN

The Bargain of Rupert Orange

I

THE MARVEL IS, THAT the memory of Rupert Orange, whose name was a signal for chatter amongst people both in Europe and America not many years ago, has now almost died out. Even in New York where he was born, and where the facts of his secret and mysterious life were most discussed, he is quite forgotten. At times, indeed, some old lady will whisper to you at dinner, that a certain young man reminds her of Rupert Orange, only he is not so handsome; but she is one of those who keep the mere incidents of their past much more brightly polished than the important things of their present. The men who worshipped him, who copied his clothes, his walk, his mode of pronouncing words, and his manner of saying things, stare vaguely when he is mentioned. And the other day at a well-known club I was having some general talk with a man whose black hair is shot with white, when he exclaimed somewhat suddenly: "How little one hears about Rupert Orange now!" and then added: "I wonder what became of him?" As to the first part of this speech I kept my mouth resolutely shut; for how could I deny his saying, since I had lately seen a weed-covered grave with the early moss growing into the letters on the headstone? As to the second part, it is now my business to set forth the answer to that: and I think when the fire begins to blaze it will lighten certain recollections which have become dark. Of course, there are numberless people who never heard the story of Rupert Orange; but there are also crowds of men and women who followed his brilliant life with intense interest, while his shameful death will be in many a one's remembrance.

The knowledge of this case I got over a year ago; and I would have written then, had my hands been free. But there has recently died at Vienna the Countess de Volnay, whose notorious connection with Orange was at one time the subject of every man's bruit. Her I met two years since in Paris, where she was living like a work-woman. I learned that she had sold her house, and her goods she had given to the poor.

She was still a remarkable woman, though her great beauty had faded, and despite a restless, terrified manner, which gave one the monstrous idea that she always felt the devil looking over her shoulder. Her hair was white as paper, and yet she was far from the age when women cease to grin in ball-rooms. A great fear seemed to have sprung to her face and been paralysed there: a fear which could be detected in her shaking voice. It was from her that I learned certain primary facts of this narration; and she cried to me not to publish them till I heard of her death—as a man on the gallows sometimes asks the hangman not to adjust the noose too tight round his neck. I am altogether sure that what Orange himself told her, he never told any one else. I wish I had her running tongue instead of my slow pen, and then I would not be writing slovenly and clumsily, doubtless, for the relation; vainly, I am afraid, for the moral.

Now Rupert Orange lived with his aunt in New York till he was twenty-four years old, and when she died, leaving her entire estate to him, a furious contest arose over the will. Principal in the contest was Mrs. Annice, the wife of a discarded nephew; and she prosecuted the cause with the pertinacity and virulence which we often find in women of thirty. So good a pursuivant did she prove, that she and her husband leaped suddenly from indigence to great wealth: for the Court declared that the old lady had died lunatic; that she had been unduly influenced; and, that consequently her testament was void. But this decision, which raised them up, brought Rupert to the ground. There is no worse fall than the fall of a man from opulence to poverty; and Rupert, after his luxurious rearing, had to undergo this fall. Yet he had the vigour and confidence of the young. His little verses and sonnets had been praised when he was an amateur; now he undertook to make his pen a bread-winner—with the direst results. At first, nothing would do him but the great magazines; and from these, week after week, he received back his really clever articles, accompanied by cold refusals. Then for months he hung about the offices of every outcast paper, waiting for the editor. When at length the editor did come, he generally told Rupert that he had promised all his outlying work to some bar-room acquaintance. So push by push he was brought to his knees; and finally he dared not walk out till nightfall, for fear some of those who knew him in prosperity might witness his destitution.

One night early in December, about six o'clock, he left the mean flat-house on the west side of the city in which he occupied one room, and started (as they say in New York) "up town." The snow had frozen in lumps, and the gas lamps gleamed warmly on it for the man who had not seen a fire in months. When he reached Fifty-ninth Street, he turned east and skirted Central Park till he came to the Fifth Avenue. And here a sudden fancy seized him to walk this street, which shame and pride had kept him off since his downfall. He had not proceeded far, when he was stopped by an old man.

"Can you tell me, sir," says the old man, politely, "if this street runs on further than Central Park?"

"Oh, yes," answered Rupert, scraping at his throat; for he had not spoken to a soul for five days, and the phlegm had gathered. "It goes up a considerable distance from here."

"You'll forgive me asking you," went on the ancient. "I am only passing through the city, and I want to find out all I can."

"You're quite welcome," said Orange. "That," he added, pointing, "is St. Luke's Hospital."

They spoke a few more sentences, then as the stranger turned "down town," Rupert fell in with his walk. He did this partly because he was craving for fellowship; partly, too, from that feeling which certain men have—men who have never done anything for themselves in this world, and never will do anything—that distant relations, and even total strangers, are apt at any moment to fling fortunes into their hands. As they proceeded along the avenue, Orange turned to survey his companion. A shrewd wind was blowing, and it tossed the old gentleman's long beard over his shoulder, and ruffled the white hair under his soft hat. His clothes were plain, even shabby; and he had an odd trick of planting his feet on the ground without bending his knees, as though his legs were broomsticks. Orange thought, bitterly enough! how short a time had passed since the days when he would have taken poison as an alternative to walking down the Fifth Avenue with such an associate. Now they were equal: or indeed the old man was the better off of the two: for if he wore impossible broad-toed boots, Orange had to stamp his feet to keep the cold from striking through his worn-out shoes. What cared he for the criticism of the smart, well-fed "Society" now, when numbers of that far greater society, of which he was one, were starving in garrets! As he thought these things, a late afternoon reception began to pour out its crowds, and a young man and a girl, who had known Rupert in the days of his prosperity, came forth and glared with contempt at the two mean passengers. Not a muscle in Rupert's face quivered: he even afforded those two the tribute of a sneer.

When the pair of walkers reached Thirty-fourth Street they switched into Broadway. A silence had fallen between them, and it was in silence they paraded the thoroughfare. Here all was garish light and glare: carriages darted to and fro, restaurants were thronged, theatres ablaze, women smiling: everything told of a great city starting a night of pleasure. Besides the love of pleasure which was his main characteristic, Orange was distinctly gregarious; and the sight of all this joy, which he had once revelled in himself, struck like a knife into his hungry, lonely heart. At that moment he thought he would give his very soul to get some money.

"All these people seem happy," says the old man, suddenly.

"Yes," replied Orange. "*They* are happy enough!"

The old man caught the reply, and noticed the sour twang in it. He looked up quickly and saw that Rupert's eyes watered.

"Why, man," he exclaimed, "I believe you're crying! or perhaps you're cold! Come in here, come right in to the Hoffman House!" he went on, tugging at Rupert's coat.

Rupert hesitated. The sensitiveness of one who had never taken a favour which he could not repay, held him back. But the desire for warmth and sympathy prevailed, so he entered. The usual crowd of loafers was about the bar, and those who composed it looked scoffingly at Orange's shiny overcoat and time-eaten trousers. Believe me, the man in rags is not half so pitiable as the poor creature who tries to maintain the appearance of a gentleman: the man who inks seams by night which grow all white by day; who keeps his fingers close pressed to his palm lest the rents in his glove be seen; who walks with his arm across his breast for fear his coat should fly open and proclaim its lack of buttons. Even the waiters looked disparagingly at Orange; and a waiter's jibes, or any flunkey's, are, perhaps, the sorest of all. But the old man, without noticing, sat down at a table and ordered a bottle of champagne. When the wine was brought, the two sat together some time in a muse. Then, of a sudden, the greybeard broke out.

"Wealth!" he cried, staring into Rupert's eyes, "wealth is the only thing worth striving for in this world! Your tub-philosophers may laugh at it, but they only laugh to keep away from themselves a can-kering envy and desire which would be more bitter than their present lack. Let any man whom you call a genius arrive at this hotel tonight, and let a millionaire arrive at the same moment, and I'll bet you the millionaire gets the attention every time! A millionaire travels round the earth, and he gets respect everywhere he goes—why? Because he buys it. That's the way to get respect in the nineteenth century—buy it! Do the fine works of art which are sold each year go to the pauper student who worships them? No, sir, they go to the man who has the money, and who shells out the biggest price. I repeat, my young friend, that what's there" (and he slapped his pocket) "is what counts in the struggle of life."

"I agree with you," answered Orange, "that money counts for a great deal."

"A great deal!" repeated the other, scornfully, being now, perhaps, somewhat warmed with wine. "A great deal! what have you to offer instead? Religion? Ministers are the parasites of rich men. Art? Go into the studio of any friend of yours tomorrow, and see whom he'll speak to first—you, or the man with a cheque in his hand. Why, if a poor man had the brains of Shakespeare, or our Emerson, and was mud-splashed by the carriage wheels of a wealthy woman, the only answer to his pro-tests would be a policeman's 'move on!'"

"I know it! I know it!" cried Orange, in anguish. "I know it fifty times better than you do! I tell you I would sell my whole life now, for one year's perfect enjoyment of riches."

"Not one year," said the greybeard, leaning over the table and speak-ing so intensely that Rupert could hardly follow him. His old face had become ghastly and looked livid in contrast to the white hair. "Not one year, my boy, but five years! Think, only think, of the gloriousness of it all! This evening a despised pauper, tomorrow a rich man! Take cour-age, make up your mind to yield your life at the end of five years, and in return I will promise you, pledge you, that tomorrow morning you shall be in as sound a financial position as any man in New York."

Now it is strange that this outrageous proposal, made in the bar-room of an hotel situated in one of the most prosaic cities in the world, did not strike Rupert Orange as at all preposterous. Probably on account of his mystical, dreaming mind, he never took thought to doubt the speaker's sincereness, but at once fell to balancing the advantages and drawbacks of the scheme.

Five years! Before his young eyes they stretched out like fifty years. It did not occur to him (it rarely occurs to any young man) to hark back to the five preceding years and note how few and swift were the strides which brought him over them to this very day he was living. Five years! They lay before him all silver with sunshine, as he looked out from his present want and darkness. This was his point of view; and let us never forget this point of view when we are passing judgment on him. No doubt, if the matter had been placed before a man of wealth, he would have denied it even momentary consideration: but the smell of cooking is only disgusting to one who has dined; it is the vagrant who sniffs eagerly the air of the kitchen through the iron grating on the street. For Rupert, at this moment, money meant all the world. He was a man who hated to face the bitter things of life: and money included release from insolent creditors, from snubs and flouts, from a small, cold, dark room, and, chief of all! release from that horror which he saw drawing nearer and nearer: the gaol.

"There is one more word to be said," observed the old man, smoothly. "Leaving aside the contingency of your starving to death—which, by the way, I think very likely—there is a chance of your being run over by a cart when you leave this hotel. There is an even chance of your contracting some disease during the winter. How would you like to die in a pauper hospital, where the nurses sing as they close a dead man's eyes? Now, what I propose is, that you shall be free from any physical pain for five years."

"If I should accept," said Orange, swirling the wine round in his glass till it creamed and foamed, "I'd desire some slight ills to take the very sweetness out of life." Probably he meant, for fear that when his time came he should hate to die.

He thought again. He was like to a man who arrives suddenly at a mountain village on the feast of the Blessed Sacrament, and loitering in the street with his eyes enchanted by the tawdry decorations and festoons of the houses, forgets to look beyond at the awful mountain standing against the sky, with menacing thunder clouds about its breast. Before Orange's mind a gay and tempting pageant defiled. He thought of the travels he would be able to make, of luxurious palaces, of exquisite banquets, of priceless wines, of laughing, rapturous women. He thought, too, for he was far from being a merely sensuous man, of the first editions he could buy, of the rare gems, of dainty bindings. Sweetest of all were the thoughts, that he would be at his ease to do the best work that it was in him to do, and that he would be powerful enough to wreak his vengeance on his enemies very slowly, inch by inch. With that, like the crack of a rifle shot, came the thought of Mrs. Annice.

He sprang to his feet. "Listen!" he cried, in such a voice that the idlers at the bar turned round for a moment; but observing that no row was in progress to divert them, they fell once more to their drinking. "Listen!" cried Rupert Orange again, gripping the side of the table with one hand and pointing a shaking finger at the old man. "There is one woman alive in this city tonight who has brought me to the degradation which you witness now. She flung me to the ground, she covered me with dust, she crushed me beneath her merciless heel! Give her to me that I may lower her pride! let me see her as abject and despised as the poorest trull that walks the streets, and I swear by God Most High to make the bargain!"

The old man grasped Rupert's cold hand, and pressed it between his own feverishly hot palms. "It is an unusual taste," he murmured, glancing into Rupert's eyes, and smiling faintly.

II

Orange started "up town" with a song in his heart. Curiously enough, he had not the slightest doubt about the genuineness of the contract, nor had he the least sorrow for what he had done. It mattered little about snubs and side looks tonight: tomorrow men and women would joyfully begin pawing him and fawning. So happy was he, his blood danced through his veins so merrily, that he ran for three or four *blocks*; and once he laughed a loud laugh, which caused a policeman to menace him with a club. But this only brought him more merriment; tomorrow, if he liked, he could laugh from Central Park to Madison Square without molestation.

When he reached the mean flat-house on the west side, there was, as usual, no light in the entrance, and he saw a postman groping among the bells.

"Say, young feller!" began the postman, "do you know if any one by the name of Orange is kickin' around this blamed house?'

"I am he," said Rupert Orange, and held out his hand for the letter.

"*Yes*, you are!" answered the postman, derisively. "Now then, come off the roof and show us the bell."

Rupert indicated the place, and, as soon as the postman had dropped the letter, he whipped out his key, and to the postman's surprise unlocked the box and put the letter in his pocket.

"Well! you see my business is to deliver letters, not to give them away," said the postman, making an official distinction. "When you said you was the man, how was I to know you wasn't givin' me a steer?"

"Oh, that's all right!" replied Rupert. "Good night, my friend."

He went upstairs to his freezing little room, and sat down to think. He would not open the letter yet: his mind was too crowded to admit any new emotion. So for two hours he remained dreaming brilliant and fantastic dreams. Then he tore open the envelope. He was so poor that the gas had been turned off from his room, but by the light of a match he read a communication from Messrs. Daroll and Kettel, the lawyers, setting forth that a distant relative of his had recently died in a town in one of the Southern States, and had left him a fortune of nearly a million dollars. But Rupert knew that this million dollars was only nominal, that money would remain with him as long as he could call life his own.

The char-woman who came into his room next morning, found him asleep in the chair, with the letter open on his knee, and a smile lighting his face. But he was only a pauper, in arrears for his rent, so she struck him smartly between the shoulders with her broom.

"I believe I've been asleep," said Rupert, starting and rubbing his eyes. The woman looked at him sourly, thinking that he would have to take his next sleep in one of the parks. She began to sweep the dust in his direction till he coughed violently.

"You have been very good to me since I've been here, Mrs. Spill," Rupert continued; and, I think, without irony: he had not much idea of irony. He took from his pocket the last five-dollar bill he had in the world and gave it to her. "Please take that for your trouble."

The woman stared at him, as she would have stared had he cut his throat before her eyes. But Orange clapped on his hat and rushed out. He had not even the five cents necessary to travel down town in a *horse-car*, so he walked the distance to the office of Messrs. Daroll and Kettel, in Pine Street. He approached a fat clerk (who, decked as he was with doubtful jewellery, looked as if he were honouring the office by being in it at all), and asked if Mr. Kettel was within. Now it is something worthy of note, that I have often called on men occupied with difficult texts; or painting pictures; or writing novels; and each one had been able to let go his work at once: while, on the other hand, it is your part to await the pleasure of a clerk, till he has finished his enthralling occupation. True to his breed, the fat man kept Rupert standing before him for about three minutes, till he had elaborately finished a copy of a bill of details; and then looking up, and seeing only a shabby fellow, he asked sharply:

"Eh? What do you say?"

Rupert repeated his question.

"Yes, I guess he's in, but this is his busy day. You just sit right down there, young man, and he'll see you when he gets good and ready."

The hard knocks which Rupert had received in his contest with the world had taken out of him the self-assertion that goes with wealth: so he sat for half an hour, knowing well, meanwhile, that his clothes were a cause for laughter to the underbred and badly trained clerks. At length he somewhat timidly went over to the desk again.

"Perhaps if you would be kind enough to take my name in to Mr. Kettel—"

"Oh, look here, you make me tired!" exclaimed the fat clerk, irritably. "Didn't I tell you that he was busy? Now, I don't want to see you monkeying round this desk any more! If you don't want to wait, why the walking's pretty good!—This young man says he wants to see you," he added, as Mr. Kettel came out of his private room.

"Well, sir, what do you want today?" asked Mr. Kettel, with that most offensive tone and air which some misguided men imagine will impress the spectator as a manner for the man of great affairs. "You had better call round some other time; we're not able to attend—" he was going on, when he happened to look narrowly into Rupert's face, and his manner changed in a second. "Why, my dear boy, how are you! it's so long since I've seen you, that I didn't know you at first. And, how you've changed!" he went on, and could not help a glance at Rupert's shabby dress; for he was quite ignoble. Then this remark seeming of questionable taste even to him, he cried heartily: "But come into my private room, and we can have a good long chat!" And in he went, with Rupert at his heels, leaving the fat clerk at gaze.

In a week Rupert was once more dawdling about clubs, and attending those social functions which go to make up what is called "a Season." Above all, he was listening to an appalling variety of apologetic lies. To the average man who said: "We didn't know when on earth you were coming back from Europe, my dear fellow; how did you like it over there?" he could answer with a grave face; but the women were different. One particular afternoon he was at a reception, when he heard a lady near him remark in clear accents to her friend: "You can't think how we missed that dear Mr. Orange while he was away in Africa!" and this struck Rupert as so grotesque that he apparently laughed. Amid this social intercourse, however, he avoided sedulously a meeting with Mrs. Annice; he had decided not to see her for a while. Indeed, it was not till an evening late in February, after dinner, that he took a cab to her house near Washington Square. He found her at home, and had not waited a minute before she came into the room. She was a tall woman, and wonderfully handsome by gaslight; but she had that tiresome habit, which many women have, of talking intensely—in *italics*, as it were: a habit found generally in women ill brought up—women without control of their feelings, or command of the expression of them.

"My dear, dear Rupert, how glad I am to see you," she exclaimed, throwing a white fluffy cloak off her bare shoulders, and holding out both hands as she glided towards him. "It is so long, that I really thought we were never going to see you again. But I am so glad. And how very fortunate that legacy was for you—just when I suppose you were working fearfully hard. I was quite delighted when I heard of it, and my husband too. He would have been so pleased to have seen you, but he is dining out tonight."

There was a tone of too much hypocrisy about all this, and Rupert made full allowance for it. He chatted in his easy way about his good fortune, and recited some details.

"I suppose there is not the slightest possibility of a flaw in the will?" says Mrs. Annice, regarding him keenly. The lines round her mouth had become hard, but she kept on smiling: she had some traits like Macbeth's wife.

Orange laughed his bright, merry laugh which so few could resist. "Oh no, I think it's all right this time!" he said, and looked at her steadfastly with his fine eyes.

Mrs. Annice suddenly flushed, and then shuddered. Her heart began to throb, her head to whirl. What was the matter with her? What was this cursed sensation which was mastering her? She, with her self-poise, her deliberateness, her calculation, was, in the flash of an eye, brought to feel towards this man, whom but a moment ago she had hated more than any one in the world, as she had never felt towards man before. It was not love, this wretched thraldom, it was not even admiration; it was a wild desire to abnegate herself, annihilate herself, in this man's personality; to become his bond-woman, the slave of his controlling will. She drove the nails into her palms, and crushed her lips between her teeth, as she rose to her feet and made one desperate try for victory.

"I was just going to the opera when you came in, Rupert," she said; "won't you come in my box?"—and her voice had so changed, there was such a note of tenderness and desire in it, that it seemed as if she had exposed her soul. But even in her disorganized state she was conscious that there would be a certain distinction in appearing at the opera with the re-edified Rupert Orange.

Rupert murmured something about the opera being such a bore, and at that moment the footman announced the carriage.

"Won't you come?" asked Mrs. Annice, standing with her white hand resting on the back of a chair.

"I think not," answered Rupert, with a smile.

She dismissed the carriage. As soon as the servant had gone she tried to make some trivial remark, and, half turning, looked at Orange, who rose. For an instant those two stood gazing into each other's eyes with God knows what hell in their hearts, and then, with a little cry, that was half a sob, she flung her arms about his neck, and pressed her kisses on his lips.

III

Yesterday afternoon I took from amongst my books a novel of Rupert Orange, and as I turned over the leaves, I fell to pondering how difficult it is to obtain any of his works today, while but a few years ago all the world was reading them; and to lose myself in amaze at our former rapturous and enthusiastic admiration of his literary art, his wit, his pathos. For in truth his art is a very tawdry art to my present liking; his wit is rather stale, his pathos a little vulgar. And the charm has likewise gone out of his poetry: even his "Chaunt of the Storm-Witch," which we were used to think so melodious and sonorous, now fails to please. To explain the precise effect which his poetry has upon me now, I am forced to resort to a somewhat unhappy figure; I am forced to say that his poetry has an effect on me like *sifted ashes!* I cannot in the least explain this figure; and if it fail to convey any idea to the reader, I am afraid the failure must be set down to my clumsy writing. And yet what praise we all bestowed on these works of Rupert Orange! How eagerly we watched for them to appear; how we prized them; with what zeal we studied the newspapers for details of his interesting and successful life!

A particular account of that brilliant and successful life it would ill become me to chronicle, even if I were so minded: it was with no purpose of relating his social and literary triumphs, his continual victories during five years in the two fields he had chosen to conquer, that I started to write. But in dwelling on his life, we must not forget to take account of these triumphs. They were very rare, very proud, very precious triumphs, both in Europe and in the United States; triumphs that few men ever enjoy; triumphs which were potent enough to deaden the pallid thought of the curious limits of his life, except on three sombre occasions.

It was on the first night of a new opera at Covent Garden. Orange was in a box with a notable company, and was on the point of leaning over to whisper something amusing to the beautiful Countess of Heston, when of a sudden he shot white, and the smile left his face as if he had received a blow. On the stage a chorus had commenced in a very low tone of passionate entreaty; by degrees it swelled louder and louder, till it burst forth into a tremendous agonized prayer for pity and pardon. As Orange listened, such a dreary sense of the littleness of life, such an awful fear of death, sang through his brain, that he grew sick, and shivered in a cold sweat.

"Why, I'm afraid Mr. Orange is ill!" exclaimed the Countess.

"No, no!" muttered Orange, groping for his hat. "Only a little faint; want some air!—I tell you I want some air!" he broke out in a voice that was like a frightened cry, as he fumbled with the door of the box.

A certain man with a kind heart followed him into the *foyer.*

"Can I do anything for you, old chap?"

"Yes; in the name of God leave me alone!" replied Orange; and he said it in such a tone, and with a face so frightfully contorted, that those standing about fell back feeling queer, and the questioner returned to the box very gravely, and thought on his soul for the rest of the evening.

But Orange rushed out, and he hailed a hansom, and he drove till the cabman refused to drive any more; and then he walked; and it was not till he found himself on Putney Heath in his evening dress, at half-past twelve the next day, that the devil left him.

About two years after this occurrence he was wandering one Sunday evening in Chelsea, and hearing a church bell ring for the usual service, he decided to enter. As he sat waiting, a little girl of four or five, with her mother, came in and sat by him: and Rupert talked to the child in his quaint, winning way, and so won her, that when the service began she continued to cling to his hand. After a while the sermon commenced, and the preacher, taking for his text the words: "*And he died*," from the fifth chapter of Genesis, tried to set forth the suddenness and unwelcomeness of death, even to the long-lived patriarchs, and its increased suddenness and unwelcomeness to most of us. The sermon I suppose, was dull and commonplace enough, but if the speaker had verily seen into the mind of one of his listeners, the effect could not have been more disastrous. Orange waited till the torture became unbearable, till he could actually feel the horrid, stifling weight of earth pressing him down in his coffin, and keeping him there for ages and ages: then with a heavy groan he started up, and rushed forth with such vehemence, that he knocked down and trampled on the little girl, in his haste to get out of sight of the white faces of people scared at his face, and the child's sad cry was borne to him out in the dark street.

The third occasion on which this sense of despair and loss oppressed him, was at a time when he was near a rugged coast. One stormy day he rode to a certain promontory, and came suddenly in sight of the great sea. As he stood watching a lonely gull, that strained, and swooped, and dipped in the surge, while the rain drizzled, and the wind whined through the long grass, the futility of his life stung him, and he hid his face in his horse's mane and wept.

But sorest of all was the thought that he might really have won a certain fame, an easy fortune, without taking on his back the fardel which, as the months went by, became so heavy. He knew that he had done some work which would have surely gained him distinction, had he but waited. Why did you not have patience? his outraged spirit and maimed life seemed to moan; a little more patience!

I must not let you think, however, that he was unhappy. In every detail the promise of the old man was punctiliously carried out. The very maladies which Orange had desired, were twisted to his advantage. Thus, when he was laid up with a sprained ankle at a hotel at Aix-les-Bains, he formed his notorious connection with Gabrielle de Volnay. It was when he was kept for a day in the house by a cold that he wrote his little comedy, *Her Ladyship's Dinner*—a comedy which, at one time, we were all so forward to praise. And on the night upon which his cab was overturned in the Sixth Avenue, New York, and he was badly cut about the head, did he not recognize in the drunken prostitute who cursed him, the erewhile brilliant Mrs. Annice? Did he not forget his pain in the exquisite knowledge that her curses were of no avail, and flout her jeeringly, brutally? Nay! when an epidemic disease broke out in a certain part of the Riviera, and the foreign population presently fled, he used his immunity from death to hold his ground and tend the sick, and so gave cause to the newspapers to proclaim the courage and devotion of Mr. Orange. And all these fortunate incidents were suddenly brought to completeness by one singular event.

It was on a winter morning, about three o'clock, that he found himself in the district of Kilburn, and noticed a crimson stain on the sky. More from indolence than from anything else he went towards the fire; but when he came in sight of it, he was startled by a somewhat strange thing. For there at a window high up in the blazing house, stood a woman with a baby in her arms, who had clearly been left to a hideous fate on account of the fierceness of the flames. With an abrupt gesture Orange flung off his cloak.

"Where can I find the chief?" he asked a man standing near, "because I'm going up!"

The fellow turned, and seeing Rupert in his evening suit, laughed derisively.

"I say, Bill!" he sings out to his mate, "this 'ere bloke says as 'ow he's goin' up!" and the other's scoffing reply struck Rupert's ears as he pushed through the crowd.

By a letter which he carried with him, or some such authority, Orange gained his request; and the next thing that the people saw was a ladder rigged, and the figure of a man ascending through clouds of smoke. Higher and higher he went, while the flames licked and sizzled around him and seared his flesh: higher and higher till he had almost reached the window, and a wild cheer burst from the crowd for such a deed of heroism. But at that moment a long tongue of flame leaped into the sky, the building tottered and then crashed down, and Orange was safely caught by some strong arms, while the woman and child met death within the ruins. Of course this affair was noised abroad the next day; and for some weeks Orange, with his hand in a sling, was a picturesque figure in several London drawing-rooms.

Now, which one of us shall say that Orange, with the tested knowledge of his exemption from death, and strong in that knowledge, deliberately did this heroic act to improve his fame, to exalt his honour? I have stated before that we must be cautious in passing judgment on him, and I must again insist on this caution. As for myself, I should be sorry to think that there is no beautiful, merciful, Spirit to note an unselfish impulse, which took no thought of glory or advertisement, and count it to the man for honesty.

But the time ran, and the years sped, until was come the last month of that fifth year, which meant the end of years for Orange. When in the days of his happiness and strength, he had dwelt on this time at all, he had planned to seek out, on the last day of the year, some mountain crag in Switzerland, and there meet death, coming in the train of the rising sun, with calm and steady eyes. Alas! now to his anguish he felt a desire, which was stronger than his will, tearing at his heart to visit once more the scene of his hardships, to look again on the place where his bargain was concluded. I make certain, from a letter of his which I have seen, that in taking passage for New York, Rupert had no idea of turning aside his doom. The *Cambria*, on which he sailed, was due to arrive at New York a full week before the end of the year; but she encountered baffling winds and seas, and it was not till the evening of the thirty-first of December that she sighted the light on Fire Island.

As the steamer went at speed towards Sandy Hook, Orange stood alone on the deck, watching the smoke from her funnel rolling seaward: of a sudden he saw rise out of the cloud, the presentment, grim and menacing, of God the Father.

IV

As the *Cambria* moved up towards the city, on the morning of New Year's day, a certain frenzy which was half insane, and a fierce loathing of familiar sights—Castle Garden, the spire of Trinity Church—took hold of Orange. He passionately cursed himself for not staying in Europe; he cursed the hour he was born; he cursed, above all! the hour in which he had made that fatal bargain. As soon as the vessel was made fast to the dock, he hastened ashore; and leaving his servant to look after his luggage, he sprang into a *hack*, and directed the driver to go "up town."

"Where to, boss?" inquired the man, looking at him curiously.

"The Hoffman House," replied Orange, before he thought. Then he cursed himself again, but he did not change the order.

I have said that the driver looked at Orange curiously; and in truth he was a strange sight. All the dignity of his demeanour was gone: his eyes were bloodshot, and his complexion a dirty yellow: he was unshorn, his tie was loose, and his collar open. His terror grew as he passed along the well-known streets: he screamed out hateful, obscene things, rolling about in the vehicle, while foam came from his mouth; and as he arrived at the hotel, in his distraction he drove his hand through the window glass, which cut him into the bone.

"An accident," he panted hoarsely to the porter who opened the door: "a slight accident! God damn you!" he yelled, "can't you see it was an accident?" and he went up the hall to the office, leaving behind him a trail of blood. The clerk at the desk, seeing his disorder, was on the point of refusing him a room; but when Orange wrote his name in the visitor's book, he smirked, and ordered the best set of apartments in the house to be made ready. To these apartments Orange retired, and sat all day in a sort of dull horror. For a sudden death he had in a measure prepared himself: he had made his bargain, he had bought his freedom from the cares which are the burthen of all men, and he knew that he must pay the debt: but for some uncertain, treacherous calamity he had not prepared. He was not fool enough to dream that the one to whom the debt was owed would relent: but before his creditor's method of exacting payment he was at a stand. He thought and thought, rubbing his face in his hands, till his head was near bursting: in a sudden spasm he fell off the chair to the floor; and that night he was lying stricken by typhoid fever.

And for weeks he lay with a fiery forehead and blazing eyes, finding the lightest covering too heavy and ice too hot. Even when the known disease seemed to have been subdued, certain strange complications arose which puzzled the physicians: amongst these a painful vomiting which racked the man's frame and left an exhaustion akin to death, and a curious loathly decay of the flesh. This last was so venomous an evil, that one of the nurses having touched the sick man in her ministrations, and neglected to immediately purify herself, within a few hours incontinently deceased. After a while, to assist these enemies of Orange, there came pneumonia. It would seem as though he were experiencing all the maladies from which he had been free during the past five years; for besides his corporal ills he had become lunatic, and he was raving. Those who tended him, used as they were to outrageous scenes, shuddered and held each other's hands when they heard him shriek his curses, and realized his abject fear of death. At times, too, they would hear him weeping softly, and whispering the broken little prayers he had learned in childhood: praying God to save him in this dark hour from the wiles of the Devil.

At length, one evening towards the end of March, the mental clearness of Orange somewhat revived, and he felt himself compelled to get up and put on his clothes. The nurse, thinking that the patient was resting quietly, and fearing the shine of the lamp might distress him, had turned it low and gone away for a little: so it was without interruption, although reeling from giddiness, and scorched with fever, that Rupert groped about till he found some garments, and his evening suit. Clad in these, and throwing a cloak over his shoulders, he went downstairs. Those whom he met, that recognized him, looked at him wonderingly and with a vague dread; but he appeared to have his understanding as well as they, and so he passed through the hall without being stopped; and going into the bar, he called for brandy. The bar-tender, to whom he was known, exclaimed in astonishment; but he got no reply from Orange, who, pouring himself out a large quantity of the fiery liquor, found it colder than the coldest iced water in his burning frame. When he had taken the brandy, he went into the street. It was a bleak seasonable night, and a bitter frost-rain was falling: but Orange went through it, as if the bitter weather was a not unwelcome coolness, although he shuddered in an ague-fit. As he stood on the corner of Twenty-third Street, his cloak thrown open, the sleet sowing down on his shirt, and the slush which covered his ankles soaking through his thin shoes, a member of his club came by and spoke to him.

"Why, good God! Orange, you don't mean to say you're out on a night like this! You must be much better—eh?" he broke off, for Orange had given him a grey look, with eyes in which there was no speculation; and the man hurried away scared and rather aghast. "These poet chaps are always queer fishes," he muttered uneasily, as he turned into the Fifth Avenue Hotel.

Of the events of terror and horror which happened on that awful night, when a human soul was paying the price of an astounding violation of the order of the universe, no man shall ever tell. Blurred, hideous, and enormous visions of *dives*, of hells where the worst scum of the town consorted, of a man who spat on him, of a woman who struck him across the face with her umbrella, calling him the foulest of names—visions such as these, and more hateful than these, presented themselves to Orange, when he found himself, at three o'clock in the morning, standing under a lamp-post in that strange district of New York called "The Village."

The rain had given way to a steady fall of snow: and as he stood there, a squalid harlot, an outcast amongst outcasts, approached, and solicited him in the usual manner.

"Come along—do!" she said, shivering: "We can get a drink at my place."

Receiving no answer, she peered into his face, and gave a cry of loathing and fear.

"Oh, look here!" she said, roughly, coughing down her disgust: "You've been drinking too much, and you've got a load. Come ahead with me and you can have a good sleep."

At that word Orange turned, and gazed at her with a vacant, dreary, silly smile. He raised his hand, and when she shrank away—"Are you afraid of me?" he said, not coarsely, but quietly, even gently, like a man talking in his sleep. Then they went on together, till they came to a dilapidated house close by the river. They entered, and turned into a dirty room lit by a flaring jet of gas.

"Now, dear; let's have some money," says the woman, "and I'll get you a nice drink."

Still no answer from Orange: only that same vacant smile, which was beginning to be horrible.

"Give me some money: do you hear!" cried the woman, stridently. Then she seized him, and went through his pockets in an accustomed style, and found three cents.

"What the hell do you mean by coming here with only this!" bellowed the woman, holding out the mean coins to Orange. She struck him; but she was very frightened, and went to the stairs.

"Say! Tom—Tommy," she called; "you'd better come down and put this loafer out!"

A great hulking man came down the stairs, and gazed for an instant at Rupert—standing under the gas-jet, with the woman plucking the studs from his shirt. For an instant the man stood, feeling sick and in a sweat; and then, by a great effort, he approached Orange, and seized him by the collar.

"Here, out you go!" he said. "We don't want none of your sort around here!" The man dragged Orange to the street door, and gave the wretch such a powerful shove, that he fell on the pavement, and rolled into the gutter.

And later in the morning, one who passed by the way found him there: dead before the squalid harlot's door.

THE SECOND BARGAIN

My Enemy and Myself

IN THE GARDEN, WHEN I was a child, I used to stare for hours at the white roses. In these there was for me a certain strangeness, which was yet quite human; for I know that I was full of sorrow if I found the petals strewn over the hushed grass. I had a terror of great waters, wild and lonely; I saw an austere dignity in the moon shining on a flat sea; things, cordage and broken spars, cast ashore by the ocean, told me wonderful, sad tales. And because my head was thick with thoughts, I had little speech; and for this I was laughed at and called stupid: "He was always a dull child," murmured my mother, bending over me, when I, in the crisis of a fever, was on the point of embarking for a vague land. As I grew older, I still dwelt within my soul, a satisfied prisoner: the complaint of huge trees in a storm; the lash and surge of breakers on an iron coast; the sound of certain words; the sight of dim colours which blend sometimes in grey sunsets; the heavy scent of some exquisite poisonous flower; a contemplation of youthful forms engaged in an unruly game;—ah! in these things also I found perfect sensation and ecstacy. Still, my tongue held to its old stubbornness: I was ever delayed by a habit of commonplace speech, a shame at exposing my thoughts. In time I won a cloud of easy acquaintance; but my awkwardness in conversation, my tendency to be maladroit,—call it what you like! always stepped between when I was about to make a friend. Then, at last, came Jacquette.

I remember that she was playing a composition by Chopin, a curious black-coloured thing, when I first came into her company; and now, even as I write, when our love is over, I hear that sombre music again. But the important matter is , that here was the person I had been seeking so long; here was the mind to meet with my mind; with her I could, at length, get out of myself (as we now say); become free. All the dear thoughts which had for years dwelt with me in close privateness, I gave to her; all my desires, all my mean hopes. Ah! the merry airs we had then: her bright laughter which, as wind, drove glumness, as foam, before it! I think I tired her of my enthusiasms and decisions; but it was so sweet to have some one to listen and understand, and she never would admit that she was tired. Nay! one morning in the apple-orchard, when the wind was turning her hair to the sunshine, she kissed me very prettily on the mouth.

After that, I forget how long it was till I came in one night and found my enemy sitting with her at the fireside. He was not my enemy then, mind you: indeed, I thought him a nice, pleasant creature, with a mighty handsome face. We became familiar: he seemed to like me, and I was sure I had gained another friend. The months glided by, and we three came to sitting together late of nights: he and Jacquette, the wise people, silent, gazing at each other; I, the fool, in the middle, talking in a youthful, impassioned way. Once I paused suddenly, and looked up, and caught a somewhat contemptuous smile peeping from the corners of Jacquette's mouth and dancing in her eyes; while he, for an answer, fell a-laughing into her face. Of course, I must have wearied them both, *bored them* (as we say) to desperation; but I was a very young man, with all the warmth and admiration of the young; and in the time of youth, a woman is always older than a man. Besides, I loved her so much, and I had such strange pleasure in loving her; that I think it was rather cruel of her to laugh.

"Why did you laugh at me?" I asked, when I was twisting a garland of wild roses for her hair.

"Oh, I didn't laugh!" she exclaimed. "Or if I did," she added, looking down with a tooth on her lip, "it must have been because I was so pleased to hear you saying beautiful words to us—poor ignorant things!"

The next day I had an affair of great importance in the town where I lived, so I told Jacquette that on account of this affair I could not go down, as my custom was, to her cottage by the sea, that night. But as the day waned, and the night closed in, I became the thrall of a longing to hear her singing voice, to play fantastic music with her delightfully. Thus it came about that it was nearly eleven o'clock when I reached the shore, and hearkened to the calling sea. There was a note of melancholy, almost a sob, in the noise of it tonight: and that, taken with a monstrous depression, filled me strangely with a desire to die—to give up life at this point! I saw a light in Jacquette's bedroom, but the rest of the little house was dark; and I was turning away, when my hand chanced to strike the door-handle, which I pushed, and found the door not locked. Let me go in! (thinks I): I shall sit awhile and dream of Jacquette, and a few chords touched softly on the piano will tell my love I am dreaming of her. Here (perhaps you will say!) I was wrong: but I was ready to welcome a servant's company, or, in spite of his growing offensiveness, my enemy's, should I find him there, rather than be alone with my saddening thoughts. The room I chose to sit in, because there was a dying fire in it, was just under Jacquette's bedroom; and ere I had sat a minute, I became conscious of voices in the room above. As soon as I made out the man's voice, a thousand serpents seemed literally to eat their way into my brain, turning my vision red; and I lay for an hour, maybe, on the carpet, fainting, and stricken, and dazed. Now, at last, after an hour I was myself, or rather more than myself, with every nerve tight as a fiddle-string, still seeing red, as I unclasped the long jack-knife, which the Greek sailor had given me, and laid it in the hollow of my hand.

I knew that it would dawn by three o'clock, so I stood quite still, only moving my tongue over my dry lips, and shaking my head to keep a sweat from running into my eyes. A cat cried in the road, and the breakers thundered against the rocks.

A little before dawn, while it was yet dark, I heard a murmur of low voices—her voice and my enemy's and then the man came down the stairs.

"Good night, my sweet love!" said Jacquette.

"O my darling, good night!" came from my enemy, and so he banged the door behind him.

One moment I paused to peer through the window, and make sure of my man. Then I fetched a run, and was on him like a panther, holding him close, with his hot breath scorching my face. Coming on him from behind, as I did, the middle finger of my left hand struck his eye, and now, as I pressed, the eye bulged out.

"My friend," he groaned, "for Christ's sake, have pity!"

"To hell with your friendship!" I said. "Much pity you had for my honour!" says I, and with that I let him have the knife in his throat, and the blood spurted over my hands hot and sticky. As soon as I could get free of his clutch, I looked up at Jacquette's bedroom window, and there she was, sure enough! in her nightdress, with the blind in her hand, gazing out. Straight up to her room I went, and flung open the door. She turned to me grey and whingeing.

"My little love——," she began.

I put my hands on my hips and spat hard into her face. Then I tramped down stairs and out of the lonely cottage.

I had not the least fear of detection: the servants slept in an out-house, and the place was too desolate for any chance passenger. I stood triumphing by the corpse of my enemy; but even as I looked the moon showed from a rift of cloud, lighting the blood, and the hue left by violent death in the features, and I ran for my life from that hideous one-eyed thing.

I came to the town, and to a house where I lay constantly, about four o'clock, in a curious trembling fit. I bathed my head and hands, however, in a heavy perfume, and then became strangely calm, and fell to thinking of the rightness of the deed. Just there was the consoling thought: certainly I had done a murder, but in doing it I had delivered punishment to a traitress and her paramour. Now that the thing was over, it was clearly my duty to forget all about it as soon as possible; and this I set myself to do, aided by a cigarette and a novel of the ingenious Miss Jane Austen. I had succeeded in my aim, I was clear-minded and very serene, when of a sudden something heavy fell against the door of my room.

"At this hour?" I murmured in surprise, and went to the door.

A body that nearly knocked me down, the dead body of a man, fell into the room, and lay, face downward, on the carpet. Then I did the one act I shall never cease to regret: From a movement of kindness, pity, curiosity, what you will! I bent down and turned over the corpse. Slowly the thing got to its feet; and my enemy, with a dry gaping wound in his throat, and his eye hanging from its socket by a bit of skin, stood before me, face to face.

"O God, have mercy!" I screamed, and beat on the wall with my hands; and again and again:—"God, have mercy!"

"You do well to ask God for mercy," says my enemy; "for you will not get much from men." He stood by the fire-place.

"I beg of you," I said, in a low, passionate voice, "I beg of you, by all you find dear, for the sake of our old friendship, to leave this place, to let me go free."

He shook his head. "For Jacquette's sake?" He laughed harshly.

"My friend," I said to my enemy, "for Christ's sake, have pity!"

"Pity you?" says he, in a jeer. "You!"

As I looked at him, I was stung into strong fury. My eyes clung to the wound in his throat, and my fingers ached to close in it—to misuse it, to maul it.

But as I sprang at him, he gave a shriek that woke the town; a shriek of fear too, let me think it at this last, like to that of a lost soul when the gates of hell have closed behind for ever: and when the people of the house rushed in, they found me kneeling by his dead body, with my knife in my enemy's throat, and his new blood, bright and wet, on my hands.

. . .

They will hang me because I loved Jacquette.

THE THIRD BARGAIN

The Business of Madame Jahn

HOW WE ALL STARED, how frightened we all were, how we passed opinions, on that morning when Gustave Herbout was found swinging by the neck from the ceiling of his bedroom! The whole *Faubourg*, even the ancient folk who had not felt a street under them for years, turned out and stood gaping at the house with amazement and loud conjecture. For why should Gustave Herbout, of all men, take to the rope? Only last week he had inherited all the money of his aunt, Madame Jahn, together with her house and the shop with the five assistants, and life looked fair enough for him. No; clearly it was not wise of Gustave to hang himself!

Besides, his aunt's death had happened at a time when Gustave was in sore straits for money. To be sure, he had his salary from the bank in which he worked; but what is a mere salary to one who (like Gustave) threw off the clerkly habit when working hours were over, to assume the dress and lounge of the accustomed *boulevardier*: while he would relate to obsequious friends vague but satisfactory stories of a Russian Prince who was his uncle, and of an extremely rich English lady to whose death he looked forward with hope. Alas! with a clerk's salary one cannot make much of a figure in Paris. It took all of that, and more, to maintain the renown he had gained amongst his acquaintance of having to his own a certain little lady with yellow hair, who danced divinely. So he was forced to depend on the presents which Madame Jahn gave him from to time to time; and for those presents he had to pay his aunt a most sedulous and irksome attention. At times, when he was almost sick from his craving for the *boulevard*, the *café*, the theatre, he would have to repair, as the day grew to an end, to our *Faubourg*, and the house behind the shop, where he would sit to an old-fashioned supper with his aunt, and listen with a sort of dull impatience while she asked him when he had last been at Confession, and told him long, dreary stories of his dead father and mother. Punctually at nine o'clock the deaf servant, who was the only person besides Madame Jahn that lived in the house, would let in the fat old priest, who came for his game of dominoes, and betake herself to bed. Then the dominoes would begin, and with them the old man's prattle, which Gustave knew so well: about his daily work, about the uselessness of all things here on earth, and the happiness and glory of the Kingdom of Heaven: and, of course, our *boulevardier* noticed, with the usual cheap sneer of the modern, that whilst the priest talked of the Kingdom of Heaven, he yet showed the greatest anxiety if he had symptoms of a cold, or any other petty malady. However, Gustave would sit there, with a hypocrite's grin and inwardly raging, till the clock chimed eleven. At that hour Madame Jahn would rise, and, if she was pleased with her nephew, would go over to her writing-desk and give him, with a rather pretty air of concealment from the priest, perhaps fifty or a hundred francs. Whereupon Gustave would bid her a manifestly affectionate good-night! and depart in the company of the priest. As soon as he could get rid of the priest, he would hasten to his favourite *cafés*, to discover that all the people worth seeing had long since grown tired of waiting, and had departed on their own affairs. The money, indeed, was a kind of consolation; but then there were nights when he did not get a *sou*. Ah! they amuse themselves in Paris, but not in this way—this is not amusing.

One cannot live a proper life upon a salary, and an occasional gift of fifty or a hundred francs. And it is not entertaining to tell men that your uncle, the Prince at Moscow, is in sorry case, and even now lies a-dying, or that the rich English lady is in the grip of a vile consumption and is momently expected to succumb, if these men only shove up their shoulders, wink at one another, and continue to present their bills. Further, the little Mademoiselle, with yellow hair, had lately shown signs of a very pretty temper, because her usual flowers and *bon-bons* were not apparent. So, since things were come to this dismal pass, Gustave fell to attending the race-meetings at Chantilly. During the first week Gustave won largely, for that is sometimes the way with ignorant men: during that week, too, the little Mademoiselle was charming, for she had her *bouquets* and boxes of *bon-bons*. But the next week Gustave lost heavily, for that is also very often the way with ignorant men: and he was thrown into the blackest despair, when one night at a place where he was used to sup, Mademoiselle took the arm of a great fellow, whom he much suspected to be a German, and tossed him a little scornful nod, as she went off.

On the evening after this had happened, he was standing, between five and six o'clock, in the *Place de la Madeleine*, blowing on his fingers and trying to plan his next move, when he heard his name called by a familiar voice, and turned to face his aunt's adviser, the priest.

"Ah! Gustave, my friend, I have just been to see a colleague of mine here!" cried the old man, pointing to the great church. "And are you going to your good aunt tonight?" he added, with a look at Gustave's neat dress.

Gustave was in a flame that the priest should have detected him in his gay clothes, for he always made a point of appearing at Madame Jahn's clad staidly in black; but he answered pleasantly enough.

"No, my Father, I'm afraid I can't tonight. You see I'm a little behind with my office-work, and I have to stay at home and catch up."

"Well! well!" said the priest, with half a sigh, "I suppose young men will always be the same. I myself can only be with her till nine o'clock tonight, because I must see a sick parishioner. But let me give you one bit of advice, my friend," he went on, taking hold of a button on Gustave's coat: "don't neglect your aunt; for, mark my words, one day everything of Madame Jahn's will be yours!" And the omnibus he was waiting for happening to swing by at that moment, he departed without another word.

Gustave strolled along the *Boulevard des Capucines* in a study. Yes; it was certain that the house, and the shop with the five assistants, would one day be his; for the priest knew all his aunt's affairs. But how soon would they be his? Madame Jahn was now hardly sixty; her mother had lived to be ninety; when she was ninety he would be—. And meanwhile, what about the numerous bills; what (above all!) about the little lady with yellow hair? He paused and struck his heel on the pavement with such force, that two men passing nudged one another and smiled. Then he made certain purchases, and set about wasting time till nine o'clock.

It is curious to consider, that although when he started out at nine o'clock, Gustave was perfectly clear as to what he meant to do, yet he was chiefly troubled by the fear that the priest had told his aunt about his fine clothes. But when he had passed through the deserted *Faubourg*, and had come to the house behind the shop, he found his aunt only very pleased to see him, and a little surprised. So he sat with her, and listened to her gentle, homely stories, and told lies about himself and his manner of life, till the clock struck eleven. Then he rose, and Madame Jahn rose too, and went to her writing-desk and opened a small drawer.

"You have been very kind to a lonely old woman tonight, my Gustave," said Madame Jahn, smiling.

"How sweet of you to say that, dearest aunt!" replied Gustave. He went over and passed his arm caressingly across her shoulders, and stabbed her in the heart.

For a full five minutes after the murder he stood still; as men often do in a great crisis when they know that any movement means decisive action. Then he started, laid hold of his hat, and made for the door. But there the stinging knowledge of his crime came to him for the first time; and he turned back into the room. Madame Jahn's bedroom candle was on a table: he lit it, and passed through a door which led from the house in to the shop. Crouching below the counters covered with white sheets, lest a streak of light on the windows might attract the observation of some passenger, he proceeded to a side entrance to the shop, unbarred and unlocked the door, and put the key in his pocket. Then, in the same crouching way, he returned to the room, and started to ransack the small drawer. The notes he scattered about the floor; but two small bags of coin went into his coat. Then he took the candle and dropped some wax on the face and hands and dress of the corpse; he spilt wax, too, over the carpet, and then he broke the candle and ground it under his foot. He even tore with long nervous fingers at the dead woman's bodice till her breasts lay exposed; and plucked out a handful of her hair and threw it on the floor to stick to the wax. When all these things had been accomplished, he went to the house door and listened. The *Faubourg* is always very quiet about twelve o'clock, and a single footstep falls on the night with a great sound. He could not hear the least noise: so he darted out and ran lightly till he came to a turning. There he fell into a sauntering walk, lit a cigarette, and hailing a passing *fiacre*, directed the man to drive to the *Pont Saint-Michel*. At the bridge he alighted, and noting that he was not eyed, he threw the key of the shop into the river. Then assuming the swagger and assurance of a half-drunken man, he marched up the *Boulevard* and entered the *Café d'Harcourt*.

The place was filled with the usual crowd of men and women of the *Quartier Latin*. Gustave looked round, and observing a young student with a flushed face who was talking eagerly about the rights of man, he sat down by him. It was his part to act quickly: so before the student had quite finished a sentence for his ear, the murderer gave him the lie. The student, however, was not so ready for a fight as Gustave had supposed; and when he began to argue again, Gustave seized a glass full of brandy and water and threw the stuff in his face. Then indeed there was a row, till the *gendarmes* interfered, and hauled Gustave to the station. At the police-station he bitterly lamented his misdeed, which he attributed to an extra glass of absinthe, and he begged the authorities to carry word of his plight to his good aunt, Madame Jahn, in our *Faubourg*. So to the house behind the shop they went, and there they found her—sitting with her breasts hanging out, her poor head clotted with blood, and a knife in her heart.

The next morning, Gustave was set free. A man and a woman, two of the five assistants in the shop, had been charged with the murder. The woman had been severely reprimanded by Madame Jahn on the day before, and the man was known to be the girl's paramour. It was the duty of the man to close at night all the entrances into the shop, save the main entrance, which was closed by Madame Jahn and her deaf servant: and the police had formed a theory (worked out with the amazing zeal and skill which cause the Paris police so often to overreach themselves!) that the man had failed to bolt one of the side doors, and had, by subtilty, got possession of the key, whereby he and his accomplice re-entered the place about midnight. Working on this theory, the police had woven a web round the two unfortunates with threads of steel; and there was little doubt, that both of them would stretch their necks under the guillotine, with full consent of press and public. At least, this was Gustave's opinion; and Gustave's opinion now went for a great deal in the *Faubourg*. Of course there were a few who murmured, that it was a good thing poor Madame Jahn had not lived to see her nephew arrested for a drunken brawler; but with full remembrance of who owned the house and shop, we were most of us inclined to say, after the priest: That if the brave Gustave had been with his aunt, the shocking affair could never have occurred. And, indeed, what had we more inspiring than the inconsolable grief he showed? Why! on the day of the funeral, when he heard the earth clatter down on the coffin-lid in *Père la Chaise*, he even swooned to the ground, and had to be carried out of the midst of the mourners. "Oh, yes," (quoth the gossips), "Gustave Herbout loved his aunt passing well!"

On the night after the funeral, Gustave was sitting alone before the fire in Madame Jahn's room, smoking and making his plans. He thought, that when all this wretched mock grief and pretence of decorum was over, he would again visit the *cafés* which he greatly savoured, and the little Mademoiselle with yellow hair would once more smile on him delicious smiles, with a gleaming regard. Thus he was thinking when the clock on the mantel-piece tinkled eleven; and at that moment a very singular thing happened. The door was suddenly opened: a girl came in, walked straight over to the writing-desk, pulled out the small drawer, and then sat staring at the man by the fire. She was distinctly beautiful; although there was a certain old-fashionedness in her peculiar silken dress, and the manner of wearing her hair. Not once did it occur to Gustave, as he gazed in terror, that he was gazing on a mortal woman: the doors were too well bolted to allow any one from outside to enter, and besides, there was a strange baffling familiarity in the face and mien of the intruder. It might have been an hour that he sat there; and then, the silence becoming too horrible, by a supreme effort of his wonderful courage he rushed out of the room and upstairs to get his hat. There in his murdered aunt's bedroom,—there, smiling at him from the wall—was a vivid presentment of the dread vision that sat below: a portrait of Madame Jahn as a young girl. He fled into the street, and walked, perhaps two miles, before he thought at all. But when he did think, he found that he was drawn against his will back to the house to see if *It* was still there: just as the police here believe a murderer is drawn to the *Morgue* to view the body of his victim. Yes; the girl was there still, with her great reproachless eyes; and throughout that solemn night Gustave, haggard and mute, sat glaring at her. Towards dawn he fell into an uneasy doze; and when he awoke with a scream, he found that the girl was gone.

At noon the next day, Gustave, heartened by several glasses of brandy, and cheered by the sunshine in the *Champs-Elysées*, endeavoured to make light of the affair. He would gladly have arranged not to go back to the house: but then people would talk so much, and he could not afford to lose any custom out of the shop. Moreover, the whole matter was only an hallucination—the effect of jaded nerves. He dined well, and went to see a musical comedy; and so contrived, that he did not return to the house till after two o'clock. There was some one waiting for him, sitting at the desk with the small drawer open: not the girl of last night, but a somewhat older woman—and the same reproachless eyes. So great was the fascination of those eyes, that, although he left the house at once, with an iron resolution not to go back, he found himself drawn under them again, and he sat through that night as he had sat through the night before, sobbing and stupidly glaring. And all day long he crouched by the fire shuddering; and all the night till eleven o'clock; and then a figure of his aunt came to him again, but always a little older and more withered. And this went on for five days; the figure that sat with him becoming older and older as the days ran, till on the sixth night he gazed through the hours at his aunt as she was on the night he killed her. On these nights he was used sometimes to start up and make for the street, swearing never to return; but always he would be dragged back to the eyes. The policemen came to know him from these night walks , and people began to notice his bad looks: these could not spring from grief, folk said, and so they thought he was leading a wild life.

On the seventh night there was a delay of about five minutes after the clock had rung eleven, before the door opened. And then—then, merciful God! the body of a woman in grave-clothes came into the room, as if borne by unseen men, and lay in the air across the writing-desk, while the small drawer flew open of its own accord. Yes; there was the shroud of the brown scapular, the prim white cap, the hands folded on the shrunken breast. Grey from slimy horror, Gustave raised himself up, and went over to look for the eyes. When he saw them pressed down with pennies, he reeled back and vomited into the grate. And blind, and sick, and loathing, he stumbled upstairs.

But as he passed by Madame Jahn's bedroom the corpse came out to meet him, with the eyes closed and the pennies pressing them down. Then, at last, reeking and dabbled with sweat, with his tongue lolling out, and the spittle running down his beard, Gustave breathed:

"Are you alive?"

"No, no!" wailed the *thing*, with a burst of awful weeping; "I have been dead many days."

THE FOURTH BARGAIN

A Study in Murder

A S I GOT OUT of a cab at Piccadilly Circus, I was hailed by Gladwin. "Just the man I was looking for!" he cried. "Let us go somewhere and have a drink."

At that moment a glass of brandy happened to be the thing I wanted; so I followed Gladwin to the Criterion readily enough. Besides, he was excited: and people are always interesting when they are excited.

"A man feels strange," said Gladwin, sitting down by a table, "when he looks around this place and thinks that everybody in it will outlive him."

"Do *you* feel like that, by any chance?" I asked, lighting a cigarette.

"Yes, I do. Let me tell you this, my friend," he went on, in his earnest, impulsive way, which was wont to become a little wearisome: "You know that I'm not much better than a pauper. Well! I'm sick of slaving away for a wretched paltry salary, and I'm going to end it all. I've thought about it for a long time, and something that happened today has quite settled it.—By the way, do you think I'm mad?"

"Oh Lord, no!" says I.

"Because I'm not. Now, you know as well as I do, that all this time, since luck has taken to using me as a football, I've been kept together by the thought of Margaret. I thought, that somehow or other, if I only pegged on, I might—Well! I have seen her today. She was kind enough to state that she could never marry me, and that her father didn't want her to see me again. She was also so good as to mention that it would be insane, considering my position, for her to marry against her father's wishes. Then she spoke of you.—Hullo! you've upset your glass! Waiter, another soda and brandy here!—As I was saying, she spoke of you. She said that her father was most anxious to have her married to you, and was doing his utmost to bring about the match. I suppose you never did have any feeling in that way for Margaret?"

"My *dear* fellow!"

"I thought not; and I told her so. Besides, I said that you were too good a friend of mine to try to step into my shoes. But she only shook her head, and went out of the room weeping. And so tonight I'm going to end it all! In your company I'm going to do everything that makes a man's life bright and merry; and then I'm going to blow the soul out of my body somewhere by the river.—You'll come with me?"

"Yes—of course!" I said, with a slight hesitation. "But what are these things that make a man's life bright and merry? Only the usual stupidities—dining, a theatre or music hall, and all that!"

"But it is these very *banalities* that I want!" exclaimed Gladwin. "I have done them so often when I was fairly happy, that I am anxious to learn what they seem like on the night when I'm going to die. Meet me for dinner at the Berkeley at half-past seven."

As I drove home to dress, I took this letter from my pocket and read it again:—

"I write to you because I know that you are such a true friend to us both, and have so much influence with my father. I need not protest that I love Mr. Gladwin with all my heart; but how can I tell him so, when my father will not even speak to him! Please, please try to do us good, to make our lives content. Perhaps you will think it a fine and great thing, to serve two creatures who can never repay you.—Margaret."

"How odd it is," says Gladwin, as we strolled towards the Empire, "that all this stir and bustle which I am in the midst of tonight, will be going on just the same tomorrow night, as though I had never existed."

"Yes," I replied; "how proud you must feel as you move amongst this commonplace throng! Dr. Johnson said, that when a man has resolved to kill himself, he may go and take the King of Prussia by the nose, at the head of his army. It is a fair question whether a man has not a right to take leave of life when it ceases to charm—to be beautiful."

"If you are so much in love with suicide," says Gladwin, rather irritably for him, "why on earth don't you do it yourself?"

"Oh! I have a great many reasons. The chief of them is, that so many people depend on my life. Take my valet, for instance. That young man supports his mother and three sisters. Now if I were to die, I should be a cause of misfortune to all of them. No; I cannot commit suicide, because of my valet."

"Of course you are right," said Gladwin, as we turned into the theatre; "and I am a fool!"

"Are you under sentence of death?" a woman asked Gladwin in the *promenade*, as it is called, of the Empire.

She laughed, and disappeared in the crowd. I turned to inspect Gladwin: and indeed he had a low look. His face was pale and wet:

there was nervousness, fatigue, even fear, in his demeanour. Seeing these things, I led the way to the bar.

"My friend, when I look around this place, with all its light and joy, it almost tempts me to give up the game," said Gladwin, with a glass of brandy in his shaking hand.

"How few people there are in the world who have the courage to give life the slip!" I murmured, as if in a study. "Men talk glibly about death being preferable to the smallest evils of our lot: but it is when people come face to face with death that they wave the white feather in a vehement and degrading fashion. There are but two sets of heroes in the world—the Anarchists and the Suicides!"

"You don't mean to say I'm a coward?" Gladwin rapped out with a flush.

"Really, I was hardly thinking of you. I have concluded that you intend to go back to your drudgery; to see Margaret—"

"You think wrong," interrupted Gladwin. "Let us get out of this damned hole—it stifles me!"

"When Margaret wept today," remarked Gladwin, as we sat to supper in the *Hôtel Continental*, "do you know I—that is, it just occurred to me, that she might love me after all!"

"One is usually deceived in these cases," I said, drawing on the table-cloth with a fork. "You *wish* her to love you, and naturally twist every unmeaning thing to your advantage."

"You know best," answered Gladwin, filling his glass. "If she loved me, you would be first to notice it. Margaret has a beautiful mind," he added after a bit, "I hope she may never be unhappy." And with that he put his hands to his face—to hide his tears, I think; because he laughed so loud the next moment. Notwithstanding this merriment, I thought it wise to purchase a small flask of brandy as we left the hotel.

"If I think of the time when I was a lad, it just takes the heart out of me!" declared Gladwin, as we walked, through quiet streets, arm-in-arm to the river. "My people were always so good to me; and the dear old place—"

He choked. "Try a little of this stuff," I said, offering my flask.

He took a long drink; and then we went on for a while in silence.

"I know I wasn't born to end like this!" he broke out suddenly. "I'm not clever, and I'm not much good any way; but I've never lied, I've never cheated, and I don't think I've ever spoken a bad word of any one.

By God, I haven't! And now nobody cares for me, and I'm being paid out like a hanged dog!"

We had come to the Embankment by this time, so I turned on him with great indignation.

"And do you think I would stand idly by and watch this performance," I exclaimed, "save that I am sure you can never continue your mean life! I am sure, too, that you could never bear the thought of Margaret in another man's arms; but from what I've heard——"

"Please don't add the last straw," he screamed out in a sort of agony; "let me die without knowing that!—You are the best friend I have ever had," he said, taking my hand, "the best friend that any fellow ever had."

I pressed his hand, with real feeling. Then I looked around, and noting that we were free from observation, I said:

"I think I will stop here, while you go on to the bridge. Never fear, old chap, I shall see the last of you,—'tis all I can do!"

"Good-bye," said Gladwin; "God bless you, my friend!"

He went forward a little; then, much to my annoyance (for I dreaded lest some should find us in company), he came back again, showing a ghastly, twitching face.

"If I thought that Margaret loved me——" he mumbled in his throat.

"She shall hear of your death," I murmured, "and she will be sorry for you!"

He nodded his head twice, as if satisfied, and went to the bridge. There he climbed upon the parapet, exploded a pistol at his face, and fell forward into the water.

"Did you see that suicide?" says I to the policeman who came running up.

"Yes, sir," answered the man, fumbling for his whistle.

"I had nothing to do with it, had I?"

He stopped short and looked at me narrowly. I fell to examining my cigarette to see if it was burning well. He was a young man, new to the police service, I should think. Doubtless I impressed him—in my favour, I mean: I do so impress people sometimes.

"You, sir!" he exclaimed, and shook his head. "Oh dear no, sir!"

"*That's* all right," I said.

And then I laughed.

THE FIFTH BARGAIN

Original Sin

"Sans cesse à mes côtés s'agite le Démon,
Il nage autour de moi comme un air impalpable;
Je l'avale, et le sens qui brûle mon poumon
Et l'emplit d'un désir éternel et coupable."

*—Les Fleurs du Mal.**

W HEN ALPHONSE D'AUBERT HAD laid down his book for the fifth time, having taken it up five times in his wrestle with his thoughts, he decided that even *L'Ennemi des Lois* could not distract him, and so, at four o'clock in the morning, he went into the streets. As he crossed the deserted *Boulevard*, a little boy drew near with a plaintive cry: "*Charité, Monsieur!*" and Alphonse, who was almost morbidly good-natured, gave him an alms, and paused for a few minutes of pleasant talk. When he fell to his walk again, he began to consider, with a sort of sick wonder, why the child who lived in his mind to such fell purpose, could not become to him as this child he had just left: as all other children,—exquisite, helpless, piteous things, craving for love and protection. Thus it was always with him: after his blackest nights he was ever in the morning at his penitentials: and when the dawn was creeping over the roofs of the houses, he forgot how feverishly he had yearned in the darkness to press his long fingers on the soft throat of a child.

Whether Alphonse was in love with Madame Dantonel or not, it may be said that she was the creature he cared most for on earth. Certainly, on her side, she looked for nothing more tender than a friendship with this somewhat strange young man, whom, in a way of motherly tenderness, she regarded, with his *bizarreries*, his exclusiveness, his superior silences, as a rather terrible child, spoilt by his excellent fortune in the world. At her house in the *Champs-Elysées* he found himself most readily at his ease: and this fact led him by the hand to the opinion, that he was never in the least happy when he was not there. She was the widow

---

* *Publisher's translation*: Always on my side stirs the Devil, / He swims around me like impalpable air; / I swallow, and feel my lungs burn / Filled with eternal guilt and desire. *Flowers of Evil*, Charles Baudelaire.

of a man who had been engaged with politics: Alphonse never troubled to inquire how engaged; only recognized the death of the political person as a relief, and as a period to the slight embarrassment with which he was wont to listen to the patriotics—an embarrassment which all forms of activity brought to his contemplative and somewhat melancholy spirit. And after that, he was never so serene, so nearly joyous, as when he was in the company of Madame Dantonel and the little Clotilde, her only child, who was now four years old.

It was on a day when he was most delightful, when he was taking life gaily, that, looking at the little girl as she played on the floor, the stunning desire came to him to take her by the throat and squeeze out her life. He took his leave in manifest disturbance; and fled into the street. He was shaking with horror: of a truth he loved this child, next to its mother, supremely; and yet, amid his disgust, he could not stifle a lust to murder her,—a thrilling satisfaction, as he thought of the life ebbing from her face while he crushed her soft round throat with his fingers. That was the first bad night of the many bad nights to come. On the following afternoon he went to the house again, to try himself—to see how he would "get on"; but within five minutes he departed, grinding his teeth and biting at his nails to keep down his passion, which was driving him to rush back to the house and slay the child before its mother's face. But after a ghastly night of torture, and sweat, and weeping, he found himself, in the morning, suddenly recovered! All his old affection for the child once more lived in his heart: the devil, it seemed, had been worsted: and it was in this glad condition that he lived for a few weeks. He had given Clotilde many presents before; but now he spent hours in the toyshops, finding a certain piety in thus eagerly buying, as though he were making good a case with his conscience. Ah, those few excellent days! How brilliant he was; how he dealt with the sunshine; how airily he tossed a salute to the passengers in the street!

But it was on a dreary afternoon, when the rain was whipping through the court-yard, as Alphonse stood talking lightly to Madame Dantonel and the child, that he suddenly knew himself to be the slave of his old passion. Oh, to crush that satin throat! He made one tremendous, straining effort, and so beat himself; but the effort was too much for his physical strength, and he fell on the floor as if dead.

When he began to get his senses, he found Madame Dantonel bending over him with a look of sharp anxiety.

"Ah, my poor friend!" she exclaimed, "but you have been very ill!"

"I have been ill, but now I am well," says Alphonse, in a thick voice. "I am going away—far away from Paris."

"Going away!" And when she got over her surprise: "But why?"

"Because I do no good here," he said, getting on his feet. "Because I find my life too narrow. I go to the *café*, I chat, I smoke cigarettes. Good. I dine, I go to the opera, to a *soirée*. My God!" he cries out, "do you call that a life? Please, my dearest friend, do not prevent me. I am going away."

She took his hand very kindly. "Go, if you wish it," she said; "but remember that you have always two friends here. Is it not so, Clotilde?"

Alphonse was taken with a hard shudder as he went out.

He decided to go to England; with an ultimate thought, perhaps, of America. He crossed the channel in wintry and boisterous weather, and when he came to Dover he was well content to lie there: postponing, gratefully enough, his arrival at London till the next day. Tired with his tossing journey, he took to his bed early; and at once fell into the profound sleep of fatigue, from which he awoke, about two o'clock, hot and trembling. The figure of the child was before him in the darkness of the room; the full throat, above all! was apparent and particular. He rolled on the bed, and tore and bit the pillows: not before had he longed with this violent frenzy to see the child stretched at his feet, looking solidly white and dead. Damp and shaking, he put on his clothes and went down to talk with the night-porter—a desperate chance under the best conditions; for a foreigner, hopeless! as he found. So he returned to his room, and opened his windows to the raining night. A strong salt wind was singing up channel; and Alphonse let it get into his hair and eyes, finding respite in this way, and a certain peace. Thus he spent the night, till the dawn came to show the grey, uneasy sea, and the grey sky. He departed, when morning had come, on board the earliest packet-boat, and that evening he found himself again in Paris.

Things having come to this point, you may ask fairly: Why did he not turn to the obvious remedy—self-destruction? Yes! But upon reflection it does not seem so likely. Indeed, upon reflection it would appear, that when a man has a desire, a fierce lust to satisfy, he prefers, however the powers of his soul may rebel, to live for the gratification of that desire, that fierce lust. Be that as it will, the man I am writing about did not contemplate suicide; did not, for a moment, glance along that road of escape. But he gave a dainty supper, to which he invited some of his male acquaintance, and a few ladies of generous virtue. There sat by him a superb creature, with gleaming shoulders and snapping black eyes; and as the mirth grew more disordered, he laid his hand on her swelling throat and tried to tempt himself to kill her in the sight of the revellers. Anyone rather than the child! But even as he thought it, the child floated before his eyes; the remembrance of the strange satiety he would feel when he had choked out her life, which he would not feel at all were he to kill this woman, caused his hand to fall listlessly to his side; and pleading a sudden dizziness, he left the merrymakers to themselves.

So on the next afternoon, we find him once more repairing to the *Champs-Elysées* and the house of Madame Dantonel. He was feeling easier today; and he discovered at Madame Dantonel's, one visitor who helped to soothe his irritated nerves. This was an old military officer: and Alphonse found his cheerfulness and honest geniality of character very pleasant. He had sat for about twenty minutes, when Madame Dantonel exclaimed:

"My poor little Clotilde! She has a cold, a slight sore throat, and this is the time when the *bonne* goes downstairs, so she will be quite alone. Forgive me if I go to her."

The time had come. "Permit me!" said Alphonse, on his feet in an instant. It was as though a stranger were talking: he could no more help the words than he could help breathing. "Pray do not deprive *Monsieur* of your company. I will go to Clotilde; it will delight me to see her, and I know the room quite well."

He hardly waited for the murmured pleasure, but ran, trembling with eagerness, up the stairs. The little girl was in bed playing with her doll, and she greeted him with a smile and a glad cry. He clenched his teeth, and squeezed and crushed her throat till the pretty tiny face became black and swollen, and the poor little frame, after a shake and a quiver, lay quite still.

As he came down, he heard Madame Dantonel say good-bye to the visitor, and the hush of her dress as she passed through the hall.

"*Mon Dieu!* how pale you look!" she cried, raising both hands. "Is anything the matter with Clotilde?"

"Clotilde is very well," says Alphonse. "But I think the room was too hot for me, and I am going away now."

"Really! so soon?" she said, genuinely sorry. And she held out her hand.

"No! please don't shake hands with me, I am not worthy!" cries Alphonse, with a wan smile, passing the matter off as a jest. "You will find Clotilde very well," he said again.

The door closed behind him. As the mother went upstairs to her child, he took his way to a chemist's shop which he knew of in the neighbourhood.

THE SIXTH BARGAIN

When I was Dead

"And yet my heart
Will not confess he owes the malady
That doth my life besiege."

—All's Well that Ends Well.

THAT WAS THE WORST of Ravenel Hall. The passages were long and gloomy, the rooms were musty and dull, even the pictures were sombre and their subjects dire. On an autumn evening, when the wind soughed and wailed through the trees in the park, and the dead leaves whistled and chattered, while the rain clamoured at the windows, small wonder that folk with gentle nerves went a-straying in their wits! An acute nervous system is a grievous burthen on the deck of a yacht under sunlit skies: at Ravenel the chain of nerves was prone to clash and jangle a funeral march. Nerves must be pampered in a tea-drinking community; and the ghost that your grandfather, with a skinful of port, could face and never tremble, sets you, in your sobriety, sweating and shivering; or, becoming scared (poor ghost!) of your bulged eyes and dropped jaw, he quenches expectation by not appearing at all. So I am left to conclude that it was tea which made my acquaintance afraid to stay at Ravenel. Even Wilvern gave over; and as he is in the Guards, and a polo player, his nerves ought to be strong enough. On the night before he went I was explaining to him my theory, that if you place some drops of human blood near you, and then concentrate your thoughts, you will after a while see before you a man or a woman who will stay with you during long hours of the night, and even meet you at unexpected places during the day. I was explaining this theory, I repeat, when he interrupted me with words, senseless enough, which sent me fencing and parrying strangers,—on my guard.

"I say, Alistair, my dear chap!" he began, "you ought to get out of this place, and go up to town and knock about a bit—you really ought, you know."

"Yes," I replied, "and get poisoned at the hotels by bad food, and at the clubs by bad talk, I suppose. No, thank you: and let me say that your care for my health enervates me."

"Well, you can do as you like," says he, rapping with his feet on the floor; "I'm hanged if I stay here after tomorrow—I'll be staring mad if I do!"

He was my last visitor. Some weeks after his departure I was sitting in the library with my drops of blood by me. I had got my theory nearly perfect by this time; but there was one difficulty.

The figure which I had ever before me, was a figure of an old woman with her hair divided in the middle; and her hair fell to her shoulders, white on one side and black on the other. She was a very complete old woman; but, alas! she was eyeless, and when I tried to construct the eyes she would shrivel and rot in my sight. But tonight I was thinking, thinking, as I had never thought before, and the eyes were just creeping into the head, when I heard a terrible crash outside as if some heavy substance had fallen. Of a sudden the door was flung open, and two maid-servants entered. They glanced at the rug under my chair, and at that they turned a sick white, cried on God, and huddled out.

"How dare you enter the library in this manner?" I demanded, sternly. No answer came back from them, so I started in pursuit. I found all the servants of the house gathered in a knot at the end of the passage.

"Mrs. Pebble," I said smartly, to the housekeeper, "I want those two women discharged tomorrow. It's an outrage! You ought to be more careful."

But she was not attending to me. Her face was distorted with terror.

"Ah dear, ah dear!" she went. "We had better all go to the library together," says she to the others.

"Am I still master of my own house, Mrs. Pebble?" I inquired, bringing my knuckles down with a bang on a table.

None of them seemed to see me or hear me: I might as well have been shrieking in a desert. I followed them down the passage, and forbade them with strong words to enter the library. But they trooped past me, and stood with a clutter round the hearth-rug. Then three or four of them began dragging and lifting, as if they were lifting a helpless body, and stumbled with their imaginary burthen over to a sofa. Old Soames, the butler, stood near.

"Poor young gentleman!" he said, with a sob; "I've knowed him since he was a baby. And to think of him being dead like this—and so young too!"

I crossed the room. "What's all this, Soames?" I cried, shaking him roughly by the shoulders. "I'm not dead, I'm here—here!" As he did not stir, I got a little scared.

"Soames, old friend," I called, "don't you know me? Don't you know the little boy you used to play with? Say I'm not dead, Soames, please, Soames!"

He stooped down and kissed the sofa. "I think one of the men ought to ride over to the village for the doctor, Mr. Soames," says Mrs. Pebble, and he shuffled out to give the order.

Now, this doctor was an ignorant dog, whom I had been forced to exclude from the house, because he went about proclaiming his belief in a saving God, at the same time that he proclaimed himself a man of science. He, I was resolved, should never cross my threshold, and I followed Mrs. Pebble through the house, screaming out prohibition. But I did not catch even a groan from her, not a nod of the head nor cast of the eye, to show that she had heard.

I met the doctor at the door of the library. "Well!" I sneered, throwing my hand in his face, "have you come to teach me some new prayers?"

He brushed by me as if he had not felt the blow, and knelt down by the sofa.

"Rupture of a vessel on the brain, I think," he says to Soames and Mrs. Pebble after a moment. "He has been dead some hours. Poor fellow! You had better telegraph for his sister, and I will send up the undertaker to arrange the body."

"You liar!" I yelled. "You whining liar! How have you the insolence to tell my servants that I am dead, when you see me here face to face?"

He was far in the passage, with Soames and Mrs. Pebble at his heels, ere I had ended, and not one of the three turned round.

All that night I sat in the library. Strangely enough, I had no wish to sleep, nor, during the time that followed, had I any craving to eat.

In the morning the men came, and although I ordered them out, they proceeded to minister about something I could not see. So all day I stayed in the library or wandered about the house, and at night the men came again, bringing with them a coffin. Then, in my humour, thinking it shame that so fine a coffin should be empty, I lay the night in it, and slept a soft, dreamless sleep—the softest sleep I have ever slept. And when the men came the next day, I rested still, and the undertaker shaved me. A strange valet!

On the evening after that, I was coming downstairs, when I noted some luggage in the hall, and so learned that my sister had arrived. I had not seen this woman since her marriage, and I loathed her more than I loathed any creature in this ill-organized world. She was very beautiful I think—tall, and dark, and straight as a ram-rod—and she had an unruly passion for scandal and dress. I suppose the reason I disliked her so intensely was, that she had a habit of making one aware of her presence when she was several yards off. At half-past nine o'clock my sister came down to the library in a very charming wrap, and I soon found that she was as insensible to my presence as the others. I trembled with rage to see her kneel down by the coffin—my coffin; but when she bent over to kiss the pillow I threw away control.

A knife which had been used to cut string was lying on a table: I seized it and drove it into her neck. She fled from the room screaming.

"Come, come!" she cried, her voice quivering with anguish, "the corpse is bleeding from the nose."

Then I cursed her.

On the morning of the third day there was a heavy fall of snow. About eleven o'clock I observed that the house was filled with blacks, and mutes, and folk of the county, who came for the obsequies. I went into the library and sat still, and waited. Soon came the men, and they closed the lid of the coffin and bore it out on their shoulders. And yet I sat, feeling rather sadly that something of mine had been taken away: I could not quite think what. For half an hour perhaps—dreaming—dreaming: and then I glided to the hall door. There was no trace left of the funeral; but after a while I sighted a black thread winding slowly across the white plain.

"I'm not dead," I moaned, and rubbed my face in the pure snow and tossed it on my neck and hair. "Sweet God, I am not dead."

THE SEVENTH BARGAIN

Hugo Raven's Hand

I

THE GIRL HAD ALWAYS been an annoyance to Hugo Raven. Even when their relations had been most intimate, he had found her petulant, wayward, at times a little morose; and now, although he had not seen her for nearly a year, the recollection of her vaguely troubled him. She had letters of his, for instance—eager, passionate letters, written in warm and unwary moments—which he regretted; and these letters, exposed just at this point of his career, might prove disastrous. "What a bother she is, that Grace Casket," he said to himself.

He sat to breakfast, one Sunday morning in summer, in his chambers in the Temple. The rooms were light and charming: a drowsy peace had settled on everything. Through the open windows the breath of the lime trees in King's Bench Walk floated in, and a humming bee would now and then hover above a bowl of wet, amber-coloured roses. He had the *Morning Post* of yesterday propped up before him, so ordered, that he could with ease read this advertisement:

> "A marriage has been arranged, and will shortly take place between Hugo Raven, Esq., of the Inner Temple, barrister-at-law, and Hilda, only daughter of Sir Matthew Chancel, Bart., of 12, Walpole Street, Mayfair, and The Priory, Little Maddon, Dorset."

He read this advertisement so often, that he noted how one of the letters in his name was a little out o f place—printed higher than the others, and he was irritated. But he thought that the advertisement, on the whole, ran very well. He leaned back in his chair, stroking his beard with his large, powerful hand, on which he wore two rings, and stared at the ceiling. Yes! certainly he had done well for himself in the world; had now, in his thirty-fifth year, reached the "home-stretch," as people say. He had been only an ordinary passman at Oxford; but when he came to town he discovered in the law, which has the reputation of being so dry, matter which for him was not dry at all. Well! just this interest of his in his subject, taken with his somewhat arrogant, overbearing (could it have been what is called *browbeating?*) manner, was found most valuable in his practice at the Bar. After a while he became accustomed, and began to be talked about; he was said to be a safe man to have on your side. Then he went a great deal into London society, with the purpose of discovering some woman who had money enough to be his wife. This girl, Hilda Chancel, he had now found. He was rather a favourite with people. Sometimes he engaged a little with the fine arts. He painted tiny pictures of fields, and farmhouses, and sunsets, in water-colours. He said he adored music; and in a box, at an opera of Wagner, would pass a pleasant hour in conversation. When there was nobody to talk to, he yawned and looked horribly "bored," then he told you, afterwards, how the music had charmed him. He despised men of letters, whom he called "writing chaps," and had the illusion (like many another!) that if he could only spare an hour or two a week for trifling, he could produce great books. Indeed, he used to write sugary little verses for the albums of ladies—verses about "flowers" and "showers," "heart" and "part," "kiss" and "bliss." He would read these verses to his friends, and he called them his "poems." He had met Grace Casket, who was an assistant in a milliner's shop in Regent Street, by accident, and he had made her—a girl of this class—his mistress on principle; his principle being, that an adventure which is bought is not worth having.

Hugo put his hands in his pockets, and sauntered lazily to the window. The sun gleamed on the buildings of the Temple; and all about was the stillness which makes Sunday a festival in that quiet neighbourhood. Below the window, on the gravel, some pigeons gurgled and coo'd—that strange sound of pigeons! which reminds one, in some subtle fashion, of the soft feel of warm milk. Hugo watched one of them that had gone apart from the others, strutting and pruning itself, with idle concentration; then, quite naturally, his eyes fell on Crown Office Row, and the form of a woman at the far end. He started wildly; a sick feeling came all about his heart, as if a hand had grasped him and tightened there. Then he fell to reasoning with himself. The figure in the distance had, certainly, a look of Grace Casket; but in our lives people did not appear in that way, just when you were thinking of them, as they did in silly novels and stories. He was one of those men who, having never had a taste of the marvellous, their use is, not to stand in doubt, but to deny strenuously that marvels happen. He watched the woman as she came slowly along, swinging her parasol, and stopping now and then to look over the gardens towards the river. An old gate-keeper, in his coat with brass buttons, hobbled by: she spoke to him, and he seemed to be indicating this very house. After that she came straight for the entrance.

"How absurd!" thought Hugo. "There are other men on the staircase besides myself."

He heard her slow, rather heavy step on the wooden stairs, and the hush of her dress. She knocked at his door. It was Grace Casket, sure enough. What a misfortune!

He thought of resting still, so that she might conclude he was out. She knocked again. Ah, curse her! She was sure to go to Whitcomb's rooms opposite, and ask about him. He walked with quick, hard steps, and unlocked the door.

"Oh, Hugo!"

"Come in, come in! somebody may see you."

When she entered the room, the first thing she did was to cross over and bury her face in the cool roses. Hugo thought that was rather pretty of her. She was tall and fair-formed; of the English type of prettiness—of beauty, if you will!—with her scarlet lips, her cheeks cream and red, and her waving, bronze-coloured hair. Her hands were large and covered with black gloves; when she sat down she let her hands fall together in her lap, and Hugo perceived that there was a hole in the finger of a glove. There was a note of the provinces in her speech: it came like the odour of fields in a dusty street on a hot day. Sometimes she neglected to give the letter *h* its full value; and when she observed that she had done so, she became confused, and added the letter to the next word in her mouth which began with a vowel. This habit lent a quaint effect to her talk, and it greatly annoyed Hugo Raven. "How different she is from Hilda Chancel," he thought.

She sat looking at Hugo, who was standing. "Won't you talk to me, Hugo?" asked the girl at last, a little plaintively.

"Oh, yes, of course I'll talk to you. I suppose you came here to talk," he answered, roughly. "Why *did* you come here? Will you be good enough to tell me that?"

"Hugo, dear, please don't be angry with me—I can't stand your anger!" She stood up and stretched out her arms, then drew them in and clasped her hands on her breast—a graceful, unconscious action. "I read in the paper yesterday that you are engaged to be married. I didn't know where to find you before. Oh, you can't think what I've suffered this last year! For six weeks I was so ill that I couldn't work, and I had no one to turn to. Then this morning I came here. I met an old man outside—I think he belongs here—and he showed me the house. He seemed to know you."

"Very likely!" Hugo answered abruptly. "Now then, what do you want?"

"What do I want? Oh, Hugo dearest, don't talk to me like that—you kill me! Why I want you, dear—you—you—you! You are everything in the world to me! Don't marry this other girl! No matter how nice she is, she can't love you as I do. Don't marry her—marry me!"

"Marry you? Marry a girl out of a bonnet shop? You must be mad!" he exclaimed brutally. "Great heavens! that would be a fine ending of my career. Upon my word, I congratulate you on your inspiration!"

Possibly, to endure his brutality had become a habit with her; for she went on as though he had not spoken.

"Or don't marry me, if you don't like. Only let me be near you always, never go away from you. I will be so quiet and good, and I'll try hard to improve, indeed I will. Oh, my God, how much I love you!" she cried, and began to sob.

There fell a silence. A warm air glided softly into the room and stirred the curtains. The flutter of the pigeons sounded far off. Stealthily, the sun had crept to the bowl of roses, and was drying them. In a sharp, hard tone, a clock struck the quarter.

"I suppose you are thinking," she said, wearily, "that it would be as well if I was dead."

As a matter of fact, he had been thinking of nothing whatever. He started now, and looked up.

"You know I have always liked you, Gracie," he murmured, taking a pen from the table and playing with it.

She heard him call her "Gracie," and her eyes cleared.

"Oh, Hugo, let us forget all that has happened. Let us forget this dreadful last year. Let us go on as we used to, and have our own love. I've got all your letters, and I read them sometimes and think how sweet you were. Do you remember?"

"Yes; I remember."

"Let us begin again all the dear old things—our long nights together, our walks."

"I was going to propose a walk somewhere," Hugo said. "You know Acton Green where we used to walk; we shall go there. Can you come tomorrow?"

"Ah! not tomorrow. But Tuesday—"

"Very well! on Tuesday. I will meet you there about five o'clock; I can't get away before, but the days are long, you know. And now," he added, looking at his watch, "I'm afraid I must ask you to leave me. I have two or three people coming to see me about some business matter, and I should not like them to find you here."

"Kiss me before I go, Hugo dear," she said. "You have not kissed me for so long!" He kissed her, tenderly enough. "You do love me, don't you?" she cried, clinging to him.

"You know I love you," he answered slowly.

He watched her as she went down the stairs. At the end of the first flight, she paused as if taking thought.

"On Tuesday, remember, you will be sure to come?" she called.

"On Tuesday; have I not said Tuesday?" said Hugo, with an impatient laugh, and banged his door.

II

It had become a custom with Hugo, since his engagement, to dine at Sir Matthew Chancel's house on Sunday evenings. On this Sunday, after his interview with Grace Casket, he talked a great deal. Hilda Chancel thought he was brilliant and wonderful.

Just at that time, the evening papers were packed with details of an atrocious murder. In the drawing-room, after dinner, they talked of murders. Miss Chancel loved them. She would like to know a murderer; she said murderers were adorable creatures.

"Hilda!" cried her mother.

Hilda Chancel was tall and thin, of a remarkable appearance. She had an easy temperament, a temperament which inclined her towards letting things go loosely by. She made rash little speeches, either because she thought they were clever, or because she did not think at all.

Now she laughed. "Oh, Hugo, you must help me!" she exclaimed. "Don't you simply worship murderers?"

"Ah! I am afraid I can't help you in this," he said gravely. "A murderer sins deeply against his fellow-men. I wonder how he can live after the act, how he can endure the remorse. If I were to commit a murder, I should see only one way out of the misery, and that way would be suicide."

Everybody thought that this was extremely well said. Hilda, who took her morals from him, let the topic fall. Shortly after Hugo went away.

As he was walking rapidly to his club, he was hailed in a thick and jovial voice.

"Why, Raven, old chap, I haven't seen you for an age! How d'ye do, old bird? You're not so great that you can't notice a fellow."

Hugo knew who had stopped him. "How are you, Scarford?" he said frigidly, and was for going on.

This Scarford was a doctor; a man of parts, yet a hopeless failure. He had taken a good degree in science with half of his strength, and had been, at one time, an enthusiastic scholar. Of a sudden he had become gross, and slovenly, a railer at decorum; and now he went through life unshorn and sodden-eyed. He frequented the houses of call in the Strand, consorting with second-rate actors; and knew a bar-maid at every inn between Trafalgar Square and Ludgate Circus. He and Raven had been at Harrow together, where he had often done Raven's Latin for him. During the past five years, whenever Raven sighted him in the distance, he thought it his duty to cross the street to avoid a meeting with him.

"I am in a hurry, Scarford," he said now, trying to brush past.

But the other was too quick for him, and grasped his arm. "Let us have a drink together," he stammered.

A thought shot through Hugo's head. "Where are you living now?" he asked.

"Oh, somewhere in the forest of South Kensington—you know it is a forest," says Scarford, with a loud laugh.

Hugo just smiled. "Have you a surgery there, and drugs, and all that?" he went on, to make sure that he would not be wasting his time with a sot.

"Oh yes, I suppose they are all there, unless somebody has run away with them. I say, old chap, you're much too sober, and so am I. Let us go and have a drink."

For a full hour, Hugo sat on a high stool, before a bar, drinking whisky; and was introduced to people whom he devoutly wished never to meet with again. There was a girl behind the bar, with a look remote from innocence, in whom Scarford was interested. Could it be the curious chemistry of her hair? Hugo wondered.

When, at last, they came into the open air, the doctor turned very drunk. Hugo proposed to drive home with him, and they went off in a hansom.

At his house Scarford produced more whisky; and they sat in the "surgery" drinking, and talking together. Hugo spoke of poisons. He had been reading some cases of strange, subtle poisonings lately; and he remembered one affair, in particular, which had come under his notice when he was last on circuit. He contradicted the doctor on some points, and the latter grew angry.

"You shall see for yourself!" he cried. He got up, and fetched three jars. "I've got some stuff here that will kill a horse in less than five minutes."

"How very interesting!" says Hugo, smelling at the jars. "Dear me! I had no idea. May I take a little of this? I—you see, I am a little of a chemist myself, and I should like to analyse this at my leisure."

"You may take the whole blooming lot if you like!" said Scarford, slapping his legs and laughing. "Only don't ask me to pay the undertaker. I'll go as chief mourner. To see me as chief mourner at old Raven's funeral!"—and he roared, and hic coughed, brushing the tears from his face.

Hugo went back to his chambers very gaily; and all the next day he carried a light heart. On Tuesday he was busy; and it was after six o'clock when he arrived at Acton Green. Grace Casket was waiting for him.

"How late you are!"

"How could I get here before?" he asked crossly.

Then he subdued the irritation which this girl always caused him, and went on quietly: "I came as soon as I could. I was engaged all day."

'Yes, I know, dear. I was stupid to say that!"

"Have you been here long?" he asked, not because he cared, but because he could think of nothing else to make conversation.

"Since four o'clock. I know you said five, but I had an idea that I might miss you, and I have something important to say." She looked as if she had been crying.

"Well! won't you say it now?"

gentleman, somebody else will. He's stood drinks to every man in the place, and he'll give you one, too, if you want it. What'll ye have?"

"Why, if 'e's got the money, then that's all right," answered the cabman, on whom this speech had taken effect. "If 'e pays my fare, it's no business o' mine; and I asks his parding if I've said what's a bit off. I ain't perticler who I drive, nor nobody ever said it o' me neither."

He took his drink; and, going outside, held the cab door open while Hugo stumbled into the cab. Then he climbed on the box, and the cab rattled away.

In the cab the thought of the murdered girl came once more to Hugo. He saw her face, her dress, the hands he had despised so much; in especial, he saw that last lingering look in the eyes, ere the life died out of them for ever. He beat his hands and rubbed his face—the thought was still present. He put his head out of the window; the dead face grinned at him in the darkness.

As the cab jolted along the quiet roads, he heard a hoarse voice singing a ditty which was popular at the time:

"But all the same, it is a shame
To leave a pretty maidie,
When every little gentleman
Walks home with a little lady."

It was the cabman, who was thus endeavouring to make the hour go lightly. Hugo knew the song, and bawled out the next stanza:

"At four a.m. we cuddle them,
As through the streets we're going;
'Tis ten to one we see the sun,
And hear the cocks a-crowing!
That drunken loon, the bare-faced moon,
Leaves useful corners shady,—
When every little gentleman
Walks home with a little lady."

The cab began to go slower, and then it stopped. The cabman got off the box and shoved his red, pimpled face through the open window.

"Look 'ere, guv'nor!" he said, "just drop it, will you? I don't know who you are, *nor* where you come from; and I don't want to. But I sing this 'ere song on Sundays to my missus and the kids, and I don't want to think when I'm singin' it, maybe next Sunday, that you've been a-singin' of it too. You may be balmy, or you may 'ave taken an extra drop—but, any'ow, I don't like you, that's all! If you don't take what I say, I'll set you down 'ere—it's all one to me!"

Hugo smiled greyly. "Very well! very well!" says he. "I'll do anything you want. Only get on! For the love of God," he cried, the terror which was in his soul leaping to his eyes for a moment, "get on! get on! Drive away from this cursed place. Here, I know you are a good chap—shake hands!" and he held out his hand wrapped in the stained handkerchief.

"No; I don't want any of yer blood," replied the cabman roughly: "but I suppose I'll drive you." He climbed on his box, and the cab rumbled on again.

III

Early on Thursday afternoon, Hugo Raven sat in his chambers in the Temple. He was very serene. The long, choking agony which had come on the heels of the murder, had given place to a sense of relief: and now he only thought what a benefit it was to have no more of the girl. He had eagerly scanned the papers to see if the body had been discovered: but the matter was not mentioned by any of them. It was very hot. Not a leaf stirred on the trees outside his windows, and the hum and murmur of the busy crowd beneath lulled and soothed him. How fortunate he was! He was waiting for Lady Chancel and her daughter, who had gone to see some one or other in the city, and were to pick him up on their way back. He was going to take them to a "private view," in Bond Street, of the works of a painter. He dozed. Yes: how fortunate he was!

There was a knock at the door, and Hilda and her mother entered. Hugo was immediately alert and attentive, pushing up comfortable chairs, and offering iced drinks. Hilda looked deliciously fresh and cool in a dress of some white, clinging stuff, and a large hat with drooping flowers. She drew off one of her gloves, and her thin hand reminded him of the women in Rossetti's pictures: not that he liked Rossetti's pictures; but he liked hands of that kind. They were so different from—well, no matter!

"We have just come from that horrid city," said Miss Chancel; "and it is so nice of you to give us something with ice in it, Hugo! I wonder there is any smoke left in the other parts of London: the people in the city look as if they absorbed it all."

"They *are* black, poor dears!" murmured Lady Chancel; "and they seem in such a hurry."

"On a day like this," the girl went on, "one ought to sit on a rock without clothes, like the people we shall probably see in the pictures in a few minutes, sucking cold drinks through a straw."

"My dearest Hilda!" exclaimed her mother, whose life had, by this time, become one long protest against her daughter's talk, and one long submission to her daughter's will.

"But the pictures do not suggest the whole truth," said Hugo smiling, and bending forward. "You see, there might come a time of storm."

"Yes!" sighed the girl; "I suppose one would have to keep one's clothes to provide against a storm. I don't like storms."

There came a rap at the door. "What a bother!" cried Hugo. "Pardon me a moment till I see who it is."

Two men stood in the passage. "Mr. Hugo Raven?" says one.

"Yes."

"Thank you, sir. I come from Scotland Yard. We want to see you about a girl named Grace Casket, who was found murdered on Wednesday morning in the fields near Acton."

Before Hugo could stop them, they had shoved past him into the room.

One was a tall man with an authoritative manner; the other was low-sized, with sandy hair and beard, and stupid, fish-like eyes.

"Good afternoon, ladies, "said the big man.

Hugo followed them, a little pale, but perfectly tranquil. He put his right hand, which was almost healed, into the pocket of his trousers.

"This is Lady Chancel and her daughter," he explained; "I am engaged with them. Can't you come some other time?"

"Or we can go, if you have business, Hugo," said Hilda, rising.

"I think I like the ladies to remain," says the little man.

"Yes!" added the other; "the ladies might remain. I think you said you knew this Grace Casket?" he went on, turning sharp on Hugo.

"I said nothing of the kind."

"Did you know her?"

Hugo got rather confused: the presence of Hilda and her mother was against him. "I did not," he answered.

"That's very odd!" said the little man; "because there was a letter found on her addressed to you!"

"Let us go, mother!" cried Hilda, rising again decisively.

"If you will please to stay, madam," said one of the men. "You sha'n't be kept long."

"This is monstrous!" Hugo broke out; "perfectly monstrous to keep the ladies here against their will!" He did not say more, however, lest he should have the appearance of being guilty.

"Suppose you read that letter for the gentleman, William," observed the big man.

So the little man read it, slowly, haltingly, in his squeaky voice.

"My own Hugo,
"*If I have not the courage to say what I want to tonight, I am going to send you this letter. Somehow, I don't think I shall speak to you before we part tonight. Oh, it is so hard to say! But I thought you were a little cold to me when I saw you on Sunday. But it may be my imagination. Hugo, darling, I don't know how to say it right, but if you really love this other girl more than me, take her, dear, and I shall never see you or trouble you again. I will send back all your letters if you want them, but I should like to keep them. They will be all I have of you. My own Hugo, I hope you will be always happy. Think of me sometimes. My heart is breaking.*
"*With all my love.*
"Gracie."

Hugo sat by the table, shading his face with his left hand. Then this was the important thing she had wanted to say! She had made her great renunciation, she had yielded of her own accord, and the murder was useless, after all! He felt a spasm of pity for the poor dead face; was it already beginning to rot and grow shapeless? He turned his eyes. Hilda was very white, and Lady Chancel looked old, and wrinkled, and yellow.

"Of course you did know this girl, Mr. Raven," said the detective.

"She was my mistress for three years. I had not seen her for a year. She came here on Sunday and made a scene, and to pacify her, I promised to meet her on Tuesday. I did not keep that appointment."

"Well now, that's strange!" remarked the big man. "A gentleman answering to your description spent about an hour in the *Stag of Ten* public at Willesden on Tuesday night."

"I was not the man," Hugo said, low and doggedly.

"Not? Then this gentleman, whoever he was, took a four-wheeler as far as the Marble Arch. There he discharged the four-wheeler, and took a hansom. The driver of the four-wheeler didn't like the looks of his fare, so he took the number of the hansom. The driver of the hansom has been found, and remembers perfectly driving a gentleman to the Temple from the Marble Arch, on Tuesday night. He says the gentleman was drunk. He says, too, that he heard the gate-porter say: 'Good night, Mr. Raven,' as you—that is, as the gentleman went in."

All this time the little man was edging over to the table, on the right side of Hugo. Now he knocked over, as if by chance, a valuable porcelain vase. Instinctively, Hugo plucked his hand from his pocket to save it. The little man grasped him by the wrist.

"How dare you seize my hand! You scoundrel!" yelled Hugo, losing all control. "Let go my hand."

But the little man held him with a grip like steel. "Look at the wound on this hand, ladies, please!" he called; "I want you to see this hand before it heals. The dead woman had blood in her mouth. She bit the man that murdered her."

There was a close silence. Then Hugo rose.

"Of course if you want to make evidence out of this bruise on my hand," he said, calmly, "I am naturally powerless. There is one thing, however, which will throw great light on this matter. It is in my bedroom. Let me go there: I shall return at once."

The detectives, knowing that he could not escape, agreed.

What followed passed so quickly, that no one had time to interfere. Hugo Raven came back into the room, laid his hand on the table, and then, drawing a small axe from under his coat, he sent it through his wrist. It fell with a dull thud.

"If you think my hand is such a valuable piece of evidence, gentlemen, there it is for you!" and he tossed it into the empty grate.

He gave a groan, and staggered over to the mantel-piece. "Scarford knows something, after all!" he muttered.

"He has poisoned himself," said the little man, who had been in the bedroom, "he did it well, too! He can't live more than a minute."

His eyes grew larger and larger; they seemed to start from the sockets. His tongue shot out, all black and furred. Still, he did not fall. The blood from the stump fell—drip—drip—drip—on the carpet.

www.ingramcontent.com/pod-product-compliance
Lightning Source LLC
Chambersburg PA
CBHW070352130626
46556CB00007B/3146